About the Author

Traci Grant has spent her career in education, teaching English at the high school and college levels before moving into higher education advising. She holds a BA in English and M.Ed. from the University of Washington. Having lived her whole life in Seattle, Traci loves the outdoors and finds she understands God most through his creation. After the Rotting is her first novel.

After the Rotting

Traci Grant

After the Rotting

Olympia Publishers
London

www.olympiapublishers.com

OLYMPIA PAPERBACK EDITION

A CIP catalogue record for this title is
available from the British Library.

ISBN: 978-1-80074-479-0

This is a work of fiction.
Names, characters, places and incidents originate from the writer's
imagination. Any resemblance to actual persons, living or dead, is
purely coincidental.

First Published in 2022

Olympia Publishers
Tallis House
2 Tallis Street
London
EC4Y 0AB

Printed in Great Britain

Dedication

I dedicate this book to my husband Vince. His friendship and love have been like air and water.

Acknowledgements

I have been writing this book over the spans of 25 years, so there have been many along the journey who I would like to thank for their help, encouragement, and insight. My first readers, Gail Kingma, Teresa Graff, and Kristin Jarvis Adams, were kind-hearted friends, but they provided keen critical eyes and much needed encouragement. I will be eternally grateful to my colleagues at Northwest University, and writing group partners. Lenae Nofziger read an early manuscript and helped me see holes in the plot. Chrystal Helmcke helped with the style and voice. Molly Quick saw the value in some of the tangled sentences, how they reflected how tangled Sydney felt and recognized the Scout in Sydney – one of the highest praises that I will always cherish. Clint Bryan who understood the familial dynamic and gave me ideas of how to write from different perspectives to protect. Jeremiah Webster, who wasn't a part of these writing groups, but tells me I'm a good writer, always patiently reads my poems, inspires me to keep writing, and to write better.

I am deeply grateful to my three children, Emilie, Carly, and Cole. Each in their own way have taught me how to give and receive love, not only for myself, but for them, through their honesty and full acceptance of me and themselves as the beautiful souls they are.

I would like to thank Jesus for finding me in that Sunday School classroom when I was just four years old and for never letting me go. I have never been lost, and that has made all the difference.

I would like to thank my brother and sister for letting me be the weird little sister who lived in her own head and talked more to her imaginary friends and my Mrs. Beasley doll than to them. Your friendship, then and now, means the world to me.

I would like to thank my dad for coming back and my mom for a fierce love.

In memory of my dad who left this earth for heaven on May 15, 2022. In his last days he let me know he was proud of me. My name was his last spoken word in this life, which is something I will always treasure.

Chapter One

"Mooooom. You up?" I shouted as I burst open the front door.

"Yes, of course, stop shouting," she grumped from somewhere down the hallway. "It's too early for all that energy."

"No way man," I said with even more enthusiasm, as I reached the top of the stairs of the split entry home I grew up in. "We gotta get going. We don't wanna get stuck in the holiday traffic."

"It's barely six in the morning, we're not going to get stuck in the holiday traffic. That doesn't start up until at least noon. Please stop shouting, for God's sake."

She's never been a morning person.

By then, I'd found her in the bathroom with her face crammed up against the mirror. Luckily, she turned her head in time for me to see she had what I liked to call a mid-evil torture device, otherwise known as an eyelash curler, squeezing the life out of her right eyelashes because I was about to smother her in a hug that would have likely left her with a bald right eyelid for sure. But I settled for a kiss on her left cheek that she leaned out to me.

"OK, good, I see you have your coffee, what else can I help with? We gotta be on the road in ten! We may be ahead of Seattle's holiday traffic, but what about Portland and Sacramento, and wherever else we have to drive through on our way? Huh? Bet you didn't think of that?"

"OK, if we we're going to miss all of the holiday traffic on the west coast, we needed to leave yesterday, so settle down. Ten minutes isn't going to help. I'll be ready in like fifteen." She mimicked my enthusiasm with the 'like fifteen' to mock me, but I didn't care. Nothing could quell my excitement.

"All right, but I'm going to start packing the car. Where's your bag?"

"It's in my room."

"Is it all ready to go?"

"No, I have to put my make-up in as soon as I'm done here."

"OK, let's say you're done." And I started packing up the eyelash curler and blush that were on the faded sunrise pink Formica counter top while she painstakingly put on mascara.

"Listen," and she put her hand up to stop me, "I would like to finish putting on my make-up in peace, thank you. Why don't you go pack up the snacks I have on the kitchen counter? Take those to the car, and I should be ready."

"You got it," I said with a wink.

"And settle down while you're at it. My God, girl, you're going to drive me crazy."

"I'm just excited. Road trips are fun, 'sides, I haven't seen Mark in over a year. That's a long time you know," I called as I made my way into the kitchen.

"Yes, I know. But I'm beginning to think I should have picked you up at your sorority so I could have some peace this morning."

"Aw come on, you know you miss me and my sunny, morning personality," I yelled with my head inside the cupboard where we kept bags.

She didn't answer.

As promised, by the time I had the snacks and my bag and pillow in the car, she was coming down the stairs with her bag in hand.

"Want me to drive first?" I asked.

"God, no," she said. "With the mood you're in, you'll get a ticket before we even get to Seattle."

"OK, but don't say I didn't offer," I said as I settled into the passenger seat of her navy-blue Oldsmobile for the long drive to Concord, California to watch my older brother, Mark, compete for a spot on the 1987 World Greco-Roman Wrestling Team, which was an important step on his way to his dream of representing the US in the '88 Olympic games in Seoul, Korea.

The excitement of a road trip masked my mom's anxiety. I had no way of distinguishing between her usual morning grumpiness, the thrill of a trip to California to see my brother compete in the trials, the spring before my Saturday in June wedding — and my mom's terror of revealing complicated layers of truth she was preparing to unfold for me on the way. This truth isn't something you unpack like a suitcase that just gets dumped on the laundry room floor after a vacation where you just wash the few clean with all the dirty because it's easier than sorting — and they all probably smell bad from being crammed back in the same suitcase anyway. It is more like an onion that when peeled layer of skin by layer of skin, it reveals the veins that carry the life of flavor as well as the power to burn in your eyes and nose just by their presence. And every once in a while, when I think I've washed my hands of it, I rub my eye and it sears me in ways I could never imagine.

As soon as we got on the road, my enthusiasm lost out to the monotony of the road and the rhythm of the engine. Plus, my excitement robbed me of a decent night's sleep the night before, not to mention, I got up at four thirty to be back home by five forty-five. I pulled out my pillow, laid back my seat, and with the warm spring sun painting the eastern sky the pink of dolls' lips, I quickly went to sleep.

Although she tried to be quiet, my mom's door closing woke me up. I saw her walking up a path to a brown building with three signs: Men's, Women's, and Free Coffee. We were at a rest stop, but where I had no idea.

Checking to make sure the keys were not in the ignition or on the floor so we wouldn't be locked out, I got out and locked the doors. As I stretched like a cat finally deciding to move after a long slumber, I arched my back and tilted my head hard to the right. Behind me loomed a huge, magnificent mountain in the glorious throws of spring. The top was crusted over with a glistening hat of snow, and its neck was wrapped in a scarf of bright purple, red, and yellow wild flowers. I turned to fully take it in. I don't know how long I stood there, but when my mom came up behind me, her voice startled me.

"So you're up? Oh, sorry, I didn't mean to scare you."

"It's OK. I didn't hear you coming was all. What mountain is that?"

"Mt. Hood."

"Wow, it's so beautiful. I love mountains in the spring. You know. They still have snow on them, but the flowers and grass are starting to come back."

"Yep, they're really something, aren't they? But hey, if we're going to stay ahead of that Memorial Day traffic, we better get back on the road. Do you want to use the bathroom before we go?"

"Yep, that's a good idea. I'll be quick."

Back in the car, I said, "Hey, when I get married and change my name to Hood, do you think we could make some sort of claim on this here mountain?"

We laughed before she answered, "No, sorry. I don't think the federal government is likely to give it to you and Evan, no matter what your last name is."

"Well, worth a try," I muttered as I snuggled back into my pillow.

We got gas, and got back on the freeway headed south. I didn't wake up again until we were just on the other side of the Siskiyous on the Oregon, California border.

"Wow, I'm sorry I have just slept the whole time. Do you want me to drive some?"

"No, I'm fine. I don't mind driving."

"What time is it?"

"It's one thirty, we should probably look for some lunch soon."

"Do you want to stop or just eat the snacks we packed?"

"Oh, good idea, let's just eat the snacks. I'm glad you're not going to keep your maiden name or hyphenate. It's better for you to just take Hood."

"Oh, OK. That seems kinda out of nowhere, but why is it better? I thought you'd be more liberal than that having raised us by yourself."

"Well, Rossler just doesn't mean anything to you, and I don't see why you would carry it through the rest of your life."

"Of course Rossler means something to me. It's my name and has been my entire life. It's a part of what makes me who I am. It's the name I share with Mark and Mandy." I was gaining momentum. There was something about what she said, and how she forced it out of nowhere that really hit me the wrong way, like how cold wind takes your breath away and makes you have to pee all at once. "Also, sure, I don't know Dad that well, but it is my family name. If I choose to change it, that's my choice, but I don't want to change it out of some sense of fear or archaic obligation."

"Well, marriage is not easy. It seems like if you put the independence of keeping your own name in the middle of it to begin with, you're making it harder on yourself."

"Do you really think a name is a barrier, because I think that's really old fashioned? It also allows me to remain the person I am. I'm not trying to get swallowed by Evan or marriage here."

"Well, anytime there is a barrier, it causes problems, no matter how small it seems. The tiniest of things can grow huge. You need to be as close to Evan as you can be. You can never let anything or anyone come between you. There is nothing more important than your relationship. Guard it with your life, or something will tear you apart before you can even know how to stop it."

It seemed clear to me she had been thinking about this since we left the rest stop. I didn't want to fight with her, so I thought I'd hear her out. I was starting to get defensive, and that That tends to strangle a conversation like weeds in a vegetable garden.

"Yeah, like what, how do you mean?"

"Well, when Ed and I first came back from the military. We had Mark and I was pregnant with Mandy. When we lived in Rhode Island we saved so we could buy a house when we got home. When I first married Ed, he was a great person, not the shell alcohol has burned him out to be now. He was honest and caring. He worked hard and had more common sense than anyone I have ever met. Mark worshipped him, and he Mark. Every day, when he came home from work, he put his lunch pail on the counter and drank a cup of coffee standing on the sides of his shoes leaning against the counter. There he would tell me about his day. Mark, every day, packed a bag with toys and put it on the counter next to Ed's lunch pail and drank his juice standing on the sides of his shoes while he listened to his dad.

"When we moved here, we lived with Ed's parents, Henry and Alice, while we looked for a house. Henry needed to borrow some money for something with Albert, Alice's son. Ed was ready to give him our house money. I said, 'No! You can't give them our house money. They are all alcoholics and they will never pay us back'. He gave them the money anyway. I was livid and gave him an ultimatum. I said I would never move out of their house until they paid us back the money. He said they were his family, he had to loan it to them, and there was no way they could pay us back. I said we were his family now and he needed to take care of us first. But he couldn't see his way past his duty to his father. I think it was his only source of connection to him. He knew the drink came before him, it had his entire life. But at least he came to him when he needed money and would come back if Ed gave it. It's amazing how consuming it can be to feel some connection to your dad, even if it is only to be used for money. It was enough to overshadow me and Mark in Ed's eyes."

"Anyway, two weeks went by and they did not pay back the money. One day Ed came home and said he had rented us a house and we were moving at the end of the month. I told him I would never move until the money was paid back. He said he was moving with or without me at the end of the month.

We gave each other ultimatums and neither of us would back down. The end of the month came and we moved into separate houses. That was shortly before your sister was born." She just let that sit there for a minute.

Confusion was slow to take hold of my understanding. I felt it at the top of my head, like the way fear sets in. It felt like hot liquid was seeping down my head separating my scalp from my skull and pooling up in my chest making it hard to breathe. I'm not even sure I was hearing what she was saying for a few minutes as my mind tinkered with what she'd said. "Wait a sec. If you moved into separate houses before Mandy was born, and she's three years older than I am, where did I come from?" I felt a rage slowly building in my chest that made it even harder to breathe. I started to realize this whole conversation was a set up.

"I put the wrong name on your birth certificate. Ed isn't your father, Gus is. Ed and I were separated and I was working for Gus. It was Ed's idea to give you his last name so you kids were all the same. You knew this. You saw Gus every day until you were five. You knew this. I just thought you didn't want to talk about it." She was just talking and talking. It wasn't really making sense to me.

The shock of all she was saying kept my quick temper at bay, but I could feel it building inside me like Lake Mead pressing on the Hoover Dam. My breath was short and I started gasping.

"Are you all right?" my mom asked.

"No, I don't think I'll ever be all right again," was all I could muster through the turbine of raw emotion spinning inside me. "Stop this car. I want to get out," I demanded.

"I can't stop, I'm on the freeway. Listen to me, you're way

over-reacting."

"Over-reacting," I yelled, startling us both. I had never, not once in my entire life, yelled at my mom.

"Sydney Margaret. Don't you yell at me!" she roared right back. "I am trying to have an important conversation with you, and yelling will not get us anywhere."

I spun my head away from her to look out the window at the green fields blurring by. My teeth clenched so tight, I thought I might break a tooth. When I realized I was holding my breath, I gasped for air. A few breaths calmed me enough to manage, "What do you mean by I knew this?"

"Oh, please. You were five when Gus and I broke up. Up to that point, you saw him every day and called him dad. You knew he was your dad."

"You said that. But I am telling you, I absolutely do not remember ever knowing Gus was my dad. Not at all. Obviously, this is very upsetting news to me, not just something I have been avoiding. This is something I did not know! For all these years, I did not know!" I tried to keep myself from shouting, but the words came out in a crescendo.

I stared at the side of her face, drained of color such that it looked like the pieces of cauliflower she'd cut up and put in a baggie for us to snack on. Her jaw was also now held tight as her rings clicked on the steering wheel a nervous pattern that sounded like our dogs' nails on the kitchen floor.

Finally, she began to talk again. "Ed and I were separated."

"Yeah, you said that," I cut her off. "Get to the part where I was born and then just didn't want to talk about who my dad really is." Anger barbed my every word.

She swallowed hard a few times before starting again. "I

went to work for Gus when Mandy was only six weeks old. He was just getting ready to open The Lynnwood Tavern. I was helping him get it all set up."

"You can skip to the part about deciding to put the wrong name on my birth certificate and then letting me as a five-year-old decide I just didn't want to talk about losing my dad. Why didn't you let me keep seeing him, just because you guys broke up? Why didn't you tell me who he was when you started dating again three years ago?" The questions were coming rapid fire then.

"OK, slow down. It's a long story. You're going too fast. Ed and I were separated, but still married. Gus was married too."

"Oh, so you had an affair and got pregnant with me," I spat.

She took a deep breath, "Yes, we had an affair. I knew Gus wasn't going to leave his family and that I was going to be on my own to raise you three. But really, it was Ed's idea to give you his last name. He said it would be better for everyone if all three of you kids had the same name and were raised the same."

"Did you ever stop to think how confusing that would be to me at some point? I know Gus is my dad, see him every day, but then have to figure out why my name is different?"

"Can I just tell you what happened?"

I didn't answer her. She was avoiding my question and I wasn't going to give her the satisfaction of giving her permission to, even though I knew she wouldn't answer it no matter what I said.

"Like I said, you saw Gus every day and knew him as your dad until you were five. Then, our relationship started having trouble, and I got sick of waiting for him to get his life and priorities straightened out. So I quit working for him, stopped seeing him, and got a new job."

"And you didn't think to let me maintain my relationship with my dad? Kids need their dad, you know!"

"It's more complicated than that." She looked weary, but she continued. "For a long time before this, Gus had been helping a friend of his who was the chief of police in Lynnwood. Chief Glant believed some of his officers were either selling drugs or were taking bribes from people who were selling drugs so they would look the other way. He thought Gus could help him figure it out by listening and watching at The Lynnwood. And he did. He figured out four different cops who were involved and told Glant. The officers were arrested and then tried to retaliate by setting Gus up. This was just after we broke up. I had got another job at Scott's Paper, met John, and he had just moved in with us. So, they set Gus up by sending someone to tell Gus that John was abusing you and that they would kill him to protect you. Gus hired him. But because the police were behind it, they came to us and took us to protective custody and we were all fine. But Gus was arrested and actually stood trial for attempted murder. That's why you couldn't see him anymore."

"Did he go to prison?"

"No, he was found innocent by reason of entrapment. Because the police set the whole thing up, they couldn't convict him. But that's why he wasn't a part of your life after that. John didn't want him around and he took a long time to get well and get his feet back under him."

I sat stunned for several minutes, just looking out my window to try and make sense of it all.

21

"Is that when we went to that nasty hotel and then to Aunt Marjie's house?"

"Yes, you see, you do remember," she said as if all was well and she had been right all along.

The knot in my stomach tightened and I had to clasp my hands together to keep myself from shaking.

"I remember the hotel and Aunt Marjie. I do not remember ever knowing Gus was my dad. And I cannot believe you think that letting a child decide that she just didn't want to talk about this was the right thing to do."

Shaking as it was, I put my hand on the door handle and repeated in slow and punctuated words. "Stop. This. Car."

"Please be reasonable. You can't get out on the side of the freeway. Let me get off the road and we can talk about this."

I opened the door a crack and stared straight into her eyes. The wind blowing against the cracked car door drowned out the blood pulsing in my ears.

She slowed the car, put on her blinker and moved to the right.

"Please, I'll take you to the next exit. It's just up there. I don't want you walking on the side of the freeway."

"I'll be fine."

She pulled over and stopped. Tears filled her eyes. Mine were dry and filled with rage. I got out and yanked open the back door. Pulling out my overnight bag and pillow, I slammed the doors shut and started walking down the side of the freeway. I could see the next exit ahead of me. The sign said, 'Weed, Next Exit'.

I could hear her driving behind me in the right lane, at a walking pace. All the holiday traffic we'd been trying to get ahead of was out in force and she was backing it up. Cars were passing her and honking.

She had the passenger's window rolled down and was shouting things at me. Some I could hear, some I couldn't.

"Gus had a nervous breakdown. He wasn't fit to be a dad for a long time. I thought I was doing what was best for you."

"Why are you shouting all this at me? Just leave me alone."

"That's why we couldn't see Gus anymore. Even though he was set up and found innocent, we lost contact with him. And you, you just moved on."

With that I stopped. We were on the exit ramp, and there were no cars behind her. She didn't expect me to stop, so she drove past me, but quickly stopped. I just stood there staring at the back of her car. Red lights glaring in the sun before they blinked to white and she backed up even with me.

"Please get in."

I just shook my head and started walking again as she followed along.

When I reached the small town, I went inside the first gas station just off the exit and asked the attendant if there was a bus station there. He said there was, just a few blocks away.

I made my way there, with her following me all the way.

I walked inside and started reading the schedule. There was a bus to Seattle leaving at six p.m. that night. I only had three and a half hours to wait. Thankfully, they took a check because I didn't have much cash on me. The clerk said I could go to the grocery store just down the street, and if I bought something, they'd let me write a check for forty dollars over the amount. That should give me enough to get me back home.

As I left the bus station heading to the store, my mom got out of her car.

"Where are you going?"

"What's it to you?"

"Syd, come on. You need to get back in and we can talk about this."

"I have nothing to say to you," I said as I walked away from her.

"Where are you going?" she asked, following about ten feet behind me.

"I'm going to the store to buy some food, get some cash, and then I'm taking a bus back to Seattle. There, now you know, and you can get on your way."

"I'm not leaving you here. I can't believe you're so shocked by this. You knew this until you were five. Then, Gus and I broke up and he tried to have John killed. You remember when the police came and took us into their custody to keep us safe? After that you kids stayed with Aunt Marjie and Uncle Ray for a few days. You were old enough to remember this. But you didn't want to talk about it, so we didn't push it with you."

"Yeah, you yelled all this to me. You say I was five. And you let me decide if I wanted to talk about it? That's not a decision a child should make! God, Mom. How did I come to even decide Ed was my dad? Huh? Did I come to that on my own and everyone just went with it?" I shouted back at her as I walked across the parking lot. People were staring at us like we were crazy. "I guess people will do just about anything to have a dad, huh? Some of us just don't want to talk about it and move on," I yelled sarcastically.

She lowered her head for a moment and then looked back up to yell, "You just wanted to go with your brother and sister, so I let you. It was such a hard time. I was trying to do my best for you. It was a very hard time, and you were very upset. I

24

thought I was doing what was best for you. I have always tried to do what was best for you. You tell me, what can I do?"

"You can wait until my bus leaves, but I'm getting on that bus. And if you do, you'll miss Mark's first match, and God knows you don't want that." The sarcasm in my voice was as thick as mosquitos around a summer night's porch light, and just as annoying to her.

"What do I tell Mark? He's expecting you."

I stopped walking away from her. She stopped following me. As I turned to face her, I could tell she thought I was changing my mind. I knew she'd do anything for Mark, and she always thought the same of everyone else. He was the sun in her universe. "I don't know. I'm sure you'll think of something. Lie to him. You're good at that." She looked like I'd slapped her.

And I turned and walked away. From the silence behind me, I knew she was no longer following. She was gone when I got back from the store.

When I climbed on the Greyhound bus with Seattle printed on the placard across the front windshield, I felt numb. I made my way to the back of the bus, my free hand touching each navy velvet seat as I walked half-sideways down the narrow aisle. Tucking myself against the window, I propped my pillow between the seat and the cold, tinted glass, and plopped my overnight bag beside me. As I nestled my head into my pillow, and settled in to forage through the ghosts and gods I had made into fathers who I apparently didn't want to talk about, it was time I at least thought them through. They came into my life like twilight on a summer's eve only to be swallowed, one by one, by a moonless night, black as ink. I was determined that in this process, I would not also be swallowed.

25

Chapter Two

As the bus engine roared to life, I started a list of the things I could remember from our conversation. Gus tried to kill John and the police took us into custody. I remembered that. It was the end of the summer, just before first grade, I think. John was already living with us. Seems like he'd just moved in. I'm pretty sure we already didn't like him.

John was on swing shift, which meant he slept at night, mostly, and then left by lunch time, so we had most of the day to ourselves, our friends, and whatever the neighborhood had to offer. Our elementary school was across the street from our house, but you couldn't see one from the other because there was a huge grass hill in front of the school blocking our house from the front of the school, but it was a great place to play all sorts of games. We'd spent this August day playing four-square, climbing up on the school roof and running from building to building — daring the brave among us to venture on to the skyscraper of the gym, hide and seek in the woods, and of course, lots and lots of time swinging on the bars. Finally, Mandy said, "Hey, we gotta get home so we can get our chores done before Mom gets home. Otherwise, no swimming today." We had one of those above ground pools in our back yard that drew a crowd of kids most hot days. But everyone within a mile knew, no swimming unless we had our chores done and our mom was home. It wasn't until we got to the top of the hill that we noticed my mom's pea soup green

Pinto in the driveway, which was unusual because she wasn't normally home from work for at least an hour. But it was the two police cars parked behind her car that made us run all the way to find out what was going on. When we were crossing the street, I also noticed John's F-150 was back in the driveway, even though he was supposed to be at work.

"Hey, Ma, what's up, how come you're home so early? What's with the police car? Did something happen? Did we get robbed or something?" Mark blurted out as he opened the door and ran up the stairs with Mandy and me right behind him.

"No, come on in here, you guys, we have something to tell you," she answered in a serious tone.

Mark and Mandy knew enough to be scared, but I was just curious. I looked at the officer's big belt with a gun, handcuffs, a walkie-talkie, and a whole bunch of black pockets that I was sure held really cool stuff. Then I noticed the other officers there too.

"These police officers are going to take us to a hotel for a few days. They think someone is trying to hurt John, and they need us to stay with them until they catch them. That way we will be sure to be safe."

"Oh man, the kids are coming over to swim," I complained.

"Sydney, you must understand this is not a game. It is a serious matter and we have to listen to them. You can swim another day." My mom's tone shut my complaining down like a hose on a campfire.

Her tone and my sister's crying started to get me a little worried. Mandy isn't the type to cry easily, but I knew she probably understood more than I did and so if she was scared

27

enough to cry, I should probably be scared too.

"Now I want you to each go into your rooms and pack a bag for three nights. Bring lots of books and games to play." We all left quickly. I didn't have a suitcase like Mandy or duffle bag like Mark, so I packed my pajamas, my clothes, and Mrs. Beasley in a brown paper sack and set it in the kitchen. On the way out to the car, we waved at the line of kids sitting on the hill across the street, lined up with their towels to come swimming, but not sure what to make of the police cars in our driveway, they stayed there. We loaded into my mom's car and followed the police car that was there and another police car followed behind us. I was sitting in the middle between Mark and Mandy, so I couldn't really see out. I wouldn't have known where we were going if I could. It wasn't too long before we pulled into a tiny parking lot beside a dirty looking motel. It was two stories, and all of the faded blue doors and windows were in one row facing the parking lot. The sign had a big bear in pajamas sleeping on it, but only half the lights worked.

The police already had our room ready for us, so we quickly went from our car to the door. My mom and John brought all the bags in and then the policeman drove away in her car.

"Now, listen to me. This is very serious, but you don't need to be frightened. We are safe here. The police are watching our room, and they won't let anybody near us until they find the person who wants to hurt John. We'll just sit tight in here and try to make an adventure of it. But there are some things you need to know. We are not to go out of the room. We are not to open the curtains, and we should stay away from the windows, even if the curtains are shut. Do you all understand me?"

"Yes, but why do we have to stay inside and not even look out?" Mandy wanted to know.

"Oh Mandy, I know this must seem really weird, and I don't even understand it myself. But you know how we always tell you the police are our friends, and they are here to help us if we need them? Well, right now, we need them, and this is what they want us to do so they can keep us safe."

"Who is trying to hurt John and how do you know they are?" I asked.

"We don't know who is trying to hurt John," my mom said, "but someone gave the police a clue to help them keep us safe."

There it was. She lied. She told us she didn't know who was trying to hurt John. But she did know. It was Gus.

"Can we play now?" I was getting bored with her explanation that I didn't really understand anyway.

"Yes, you can play now."

"Hey, where is my bag with Mrs. Beasley? I packed it and set in the kitchen."

"What does it look like?"

"I couldn't find a suitcase, so I used a brown sack."

"I saw that one in the kitchen, but I didn't know it was someone's clothes so I left it." John might have been truly sorry he left my bag, but I didn't believe him. He had already formed a track record of being nasty to me.

"You did it on purpose. You know I love Mrs. Beasley. I can't sleep without her. Now I don't have any clothes or any toys. I want to go back home and get her," I insisted with my arms folded across my chest. "This is all your fault anyway."

"Now, Sydney," my mom began. I could tell by the tone of her voice I wasn't going to go back, and I wasn't going to get my Mrs. Beasley. "I am sorry your bag got left. John didn't mean to leave it; he just didn't know it was your suitcase. You can wear these clothes, they won't get dirty, and I'm sure Mandy and Mark will share their toys with you."

My mom's explanation didn't help. I started to cry. I looked at the dark gold curtains that blocked me from the sunshine, from my swimming pool, from my Mrs. Beasley, and knew it was all John's fault. No wonder someone wants to hurt him. He isn't very nice, I thought to myself as I cried. It wasn't a fit throwing sort of cry. I had learned long ago not to try that with my mom. I just lay on the bed with my head buried in the scratchy bedspread covered with gold and blue flowers and let the tears come out of me.

By Sunday afternoon, the officers had come back for us. We didn't go home after we left the hotel. My mom and John drove us to Bellingham to my Uncle Ray and Aunt Marjie's house. They talked for a while, and then left.

After my mom and John left, Aunt Marjie sat down on the couch with Mark, Mandy, and me. Uncle Ray took Jeff and Greg to the park. I was mad I couldn't go too.

"But that's not fair. Why do they get to go to the park and we have to stay here on the couch? What did we do?" I was done with being cooped up and cooperating.

"You didn't do anything, Sydney, and I'll take you to the park with them in a bit, but I need to talk to you guys for a few minutes," my aunt said in a patient voice.

"Just sit down and listen, Sydney." I always did what Mark told me because he usually didn't tell me to do anything unless it was important.

Aunt Marjie's couch had a high back that curved in a little on the ends. There was wood all the way around the outside that hurt when you flopped back too hard. The material was scratchy with a lot of buttons to snag your tights on. The big blue and green flowers were faded.

"You guys need to understand something. Your mom and John had to go take care of some business, so you guys will stay here for a few days."

"Yeah well, I don't have any other clothes because John, the dummy, forgot my bag I packed," I stated as matter of fact as if I were offering the temperature outside. "And he left my Mrs. Beasley doll too." With that, my voice betrayed the growing hatred I felt for him, like my grandpa used to say, and the freight train of crap he brought with him.

"Is it about the guy who was trying to hurt John?" Mandy has always been direct. It is one of the things I admire most about her.

"Yes, it is, but that isn't what I have to tell you. I have to tell you about Gus."

"Is he OK?" Mark asked.

"Yes, he's going to be fine. But he's sick right now."

"Shouldn't we go see him and take him some soup?"

"No, Sydney, it's not that kind of sick. You see his brain is a bit sick, and mostly his heart is sick and making him really sad, and he isn't thinking quite right. He's going to go away for a while and get some help from some special doctors until he feels all better. But we can't see him for a while."

"What's wrong? Why are you guys crying?"

"Sydney, why don't I take you to the park to play with the boys now?"

"OK, but are Mark and Mandy OK?" I asked, torn between being excited to go the park and wanting to understand what was worth crying over. I had surely been with them for the last three days and Aunt Marjie didn't make us cry. As she helped me tie my shoes, I looked to Mark on the couch and he was just looking down at his hands in his lap. She opened the door to the hot August air, took my hand and gently tugged me outside. I kept my eyes on Mark, stealing a glance at Mandy, but neither of them looked up. I was beginning to worry that something was really wrong and they understood what I didn't.

"Come on sweetheart. Do you want to skip or march our way to the park?"

"I think I'd just like to walk beside you please," I finally answered.

"OK, we can do that." And she led me out the door, gently closing it behind us.

"Aunt Marjie," I asked as we walked down the street.

"What is it sweetheart?"

"I feel like I don't have a daddy anymore," I said with tears quietly rolling down my cheeks.

"Well, you can always share Uncle Ray. He loves you very much," she said gently.

"Yeah, he sure does," I agreed. "But he's not my daddy, he's Jeff and Greg's daddy. And he lives a long way away now."

"Do you remember when he was gone to Vietnam and we lived with you?"

"Yeah, that was fun."

"He was a long way away, and we didn't see him for a long time, but he was still our daddy, and he still loved us very much."

"And he came back!" I offered, with a little hope in my voice.

"Yes, he did. He came back," my aunt agreed.

"It's pretty hot today, but there's still no sunshine. Why isn't there sunshine when it's still hot?" I asked matter-of-factly.

"It's called humidity. I really hate these kinds of days. I think it's much better when there's blue sky and you can see the sun shining. I always feel like the sunshine makes me feel better and every day when I wake up, I look out my window for some blue sky before I even get up."

"I'm gonna do that too. If I can see blue sky when I wake up, I will think, it's gonna be a happy day. I already have to check to make sure it's after seven on my clock because my mom doesn't like it when I get up too early," I chattered.

"That's a good idea, sweetheart. You see if the sun is shining on you each morning, and you'll know if it's gonna be a good day right from the start."

As soon as we crossed the street and I could see Jeff and Greg, I let go of her hand and ran as fast as I could to join them on the swings.

"Hey Uncle Ray, will you give me an underdog?" I shouted.

"You got it sweetheart!"

So caught up in swinging with Jeff and Greg, I didn't see her turn and go back to her house to Mark and Mandy waiting on her scratchy couch.

Chapter Three

Riding along, I didn't even notice the stunning mountains of the Oregon-California border that had so captivated me just hours ago from the other side of I-5. So lost in my memory, I could have been anywhere and it would have mattered not. I was so baffled that I could have forgotten Gus was my dad, that I saw him all the time and knew him as dad. I tried to recall other people, events, anything from that time in my life. I started listing items in my head, trying to jar anything loose. My Mrs. Beasley doll was my constant companion. I preferred the company of my imagination to just about everybody. Really, the only friend I had was my neighbor, Lesa. Her family brought me to church with them. And then, a very clear memory came flooding back. My first day at church. It was both invigorating and embarrassing, like so many experiences to come.

Sunday School started with a game of duck-duck-goose, then we sang 'Jesus Loves the Little Children'. I didn't know the words, but I tried to join in the best I could. I moved my lips, whispering the words I heard the teacher and a few other kids singing, but I was about three words behind and skipped a lot of them. While we were sitting cross-legged on the floor covered in chocolate colored shag rugs, the teacher was sitting on a stool in the front with a felt board on her lap. The bottom of the board had green felt for the grass and the top was blue for the sky. She started to tell the story of one lost sheep, and she put a bunch of felt sheep on the board, and that Jesus would leave all the other sheep safe in their pen to go look for and bring back this one lost sheep because he loves every sheep. She put up a brown fence, a man in a bathrobe, and one sheep way outside the pen.

It wasn't until she started talking, rather than singing the name Jesus, that I realized it made me very nervous. I had heard it before, but only grown-ups said it, and I knew it was a word, like shit and the rest of the words that I said to Cocoa, our dog, in the closet when I was mad, that only grown-ups were allowed to say, and usually only when they were mad. It took me a few minutes to figure out it was the man's name in the bathrobe made of felt on the board she was holding. She had long skinny fingers, and I loved how graceful they looked as she took the felt sheep and the felt Jesus and moved them around the board as she told us the story.

When she finished the story, she put the felt board down and looked out at the small group of us and said, "When you ask Jesus to come live in your heart, he will never leave you. He will always stay with you no matter what. He will never let you be lost from him, just like this sheep because he loves each one of you. Who wants to ask Jesus to come live inside your heart?" She had not finished the sentence before my hand was in the air as high as I could raise it.

Just then, I noticed a kind-looking man with white-gray hair standing in the doorway. The woman with the graceful fingers told us we could go sit in the chairs at the tables to glue cotton balls on a piece of paper to make a picture of a sheep. As I got up she said, "Sydney, can I talk to you for a second?"

"Sure, what?" I asked as I walked over to her side.

"You raised your hand when I asked if you want to ask

Jesus into your heart. I want to ask you about that and see if you understand what that means and pray with you so you can ask him if you think you're ready," she said gently.

"Now?" I asked surprised.

"Yeah, now," she gently prodded.

"Is he here? Is that him? Cause he won't fit into my heart." I nodded my head toward the white-haired man in the doorway.

A broad smile came across both their faces as I looked from one of them to the other, and they looked at each other. "No, that is our pastor. His name is Mr. Sather, but he would probably like to join us when we pray, if you don't mind."

"Sure, does he know Jesus?"

"Yes, he does." They both smiled again.

The man with the grayish white hair sat down on the floor beside me and the lady with the graceful fingers, and asked me, "What do you know about Jesus?"

"Well, at home, that's a word only my step dad can say, and he says it a lot, especially when he's fishing and building things and drops something he needs, but he uses his last name too, you know, Christ. It's like when my mom is mad at me and she calls me Sydney Margaret. Well, John gets mad like Jesus Christ made him mess up and yells at him for it. And he does the same thing to God, but his last name is Damnit. And then just what she said today," as I pointed to the nice lady with graceful fingers. "You know, he likes to look for lost sheep, and if I ask him into my heart, he won't leave." I looked at them, satisfied.

"Yes, that is very true. But there are some other things you should know that are also true. The name part isn't quite right, but we'll work on that later. Jesus is God's son. God wants us all to live with him in heaven, but God is perfect and has never done anything bad, ever. Neither has Jesus. All of us people, we have done things that are not perfect, so we can't be in heaven unless there is some way to make up for the bad things we have done. But the thing is, we can't make up for them. We just aren't able to. So, God sent Jesus to do it for us. So, Jesus, even though he never did anything bad, died for all the bad things all people have ever done and then three days later he came back to life, and if we accept Jesus into our hearts, and ask him to forgive the bad things we have done, then we can be with God. Does that make sense to you?"

"You bet. It's like when I tell a lie and say sorry and my mom says sorry isn't good enough, you have to go to your room, but then she still seems mad even when I come out of my room, so that doesn't seem good enough either, and I need my brother to cheer her up because he's her favorite, and it seems like he never does anything bad, so she's never mad at him. So, what Jesus did is good enough? But what about the part that he won't ever leave me like what she said?"

Mr. Sather chuckled a bit. "Yes, I think you understand. What was right, he won't ever leave you."

"Oh, thank God," I sighed.

Mr. Sather said, "I'll pray and you can just repeat what I say, OK?"

"OK by me."

"Dear Jesus, please come into my heart and forgive me for my sins," he said.

"Dear Jesus, please come into my heart and forgive me for my sins," I repeated.

"Thank you for your love and that you will never leave me."

"Yep, thank you for loving me and that you won't ever leave me," I repeated.

"Amen."

I opened my eyes and looked at him. "What does that mean?"

"Oh, that means so be it. It's a word you say at the end of a prayer."

"Oh, thanks." And I closed my eyes again and said, "Amen." When I opened my eyes, I said, "Where's hell?"

He smiled and said, "That's a tough one to answer. I don't know exactly where it is, but it's a place where God is not and we don't want to be there because we can't be with God there."

I said, "That's for sure. I wanna be where God is too." And I got up, hugged him around the neck and kissed his cheek before I went to make my sheep picture with the cotton balls and glue. When I got home, I opened the door and announced in my loudest voice, "I asked Jesus into my heart, guys. I'm not a lost sheep anymore, so he won't ever leave me. You guys should too or you'll probably go to hell."

I chuckled to myself, sitting there with my face crammed up against my pillow. It was a clear memory, but not what I was looking for.

Chapter Four

At some point, I must have dosed off. The hum of the motor and monotony of the scenery fading into the darkening night partnered with my emotional exhaustion to overcome my efforts to remember ever knowing Gus was my dad. A grubby looking young guy in a sleeveless Iron Maiden t-shirt and faded Levis slammed the bathroom door, jolting me awake. It took me a few minutes to get my bearings. The tinted windows made it hard to tell just how dark it actually was outside so I had no idea what time it was or where we were or how long I'd been asleep. I looked at my watch and the glow in the dark dots let me know it was just before one in the morning. I stretched in the seat, arching my back. I decided to go to the bathroom myself. As I trudged back up the narrow aisle to my seat, I recalled the first time I went with Mark and Mandy to Ed's house.

"Hey Mandy, what ya doin'?" I asked as I pushed open the door to her room.

"I'm packin' my bag to go to Daddy's house. He's suppos' ta be here at five."

"Oh," I muttered as I hung my head and slumped into her pink beanbag chair. "What do you do there?"

"Well, sometimes we go to the drive-in movies, and sometimes we go camping, but mostly we just stay there and play with Anna, Bud, and Robby."

"Is it fun there?" I asked.

"Sometimes it is. They let us play hide and seek outside when it's dark, and that's fun because it's past bedtime. But Pat is real mean. She makes super gross food, and then you have to eat it all. If you don't, she gives it to you again for breakfast. I never eat it. Which reminds me, I have to get some snacks to sneak and eat. Hey, why are you crying, Syd?"

"I wish I could go. Aunt Marjie said I could share Uncle Ray, but he lives so far away now," I said.

"Well, why don't you come with us?" she said enthusiastically.

My head snapped up. "Do you think I could?" I asked in amazement.

"Let's go ask." As we left her room and started down the hallway, we heard a car pull into the driveway. We both stopped and looked at each other. Without saying a word, we ran into my room, jumped on my bed, and scampered to peer out the window to see Ed rounding the back of mom's green Pinto as he headed to the front door.

"Oh no," Mandy said in a panic, "we didn't get a chance to ask yet."

"Well, let's ask now," I insisted. With that, I jumped off my bed and ran down the hallway. Mark had opened the door, and Ed was just stepping inside. My mom was standing at the top of the stairs when I met her at the end of the hallway. "Hey, Mom, can I go with Mark and Mandy to Ed's house this weekend? Pretty please? Mandy said it's OK with her," I blurted out in a rush and then looked expectantly from my mom to Ed. They just stared at each other, not knowing how to answer me.

Finally, after a super long time, Ed broke the awkward silence, "Sure, Sydney. You can come with us."

"Hot damn!" I shouted full of excitement.

"Sydney Margaret!" my mom scolded. "Where did you ever hear that?"

"Grandpa Rhodes says that all the time when we watch baseball and the Yankees get a good hit," I answered matter-of-factly.

Ed was trying not to laugh as my mom explained, "Well, Grandpa shouldn't say that. It's not a nice word, and you absolutely should not say that. Do you understand me?"

"Yeah, I understand. Sorry. I just got excited." I was afraid she might not let me go, so I would say anything at that point. "Mandy," who was coming out of the kitchen with a handful of snacks, "can you help me pack my bag, too?" I said as I was turning to head to my room and get my things together.

"Hold on a sec there, little missy," my mom said. Then, turning to Ed, she said, "Are you sure about this. I don't know if this is a good idea."

He had come half way up the stairs by then and answered with confidence, "Leslie, why not? She just wants to be like her brother and sister. Can't hurt. Plus, you and John could probably use a few days. I've been following along in the paper. Things seem pretty tense."

"Yeah, we had to cancel the paper," she said giving him a look that said, enough about that.

I could tell she was thinking as she looked at me standing beside Mandy, then at Ed with Mark behind him. I just smiled at her, hoping she would say yes.

"OK, we'll give it a try," she finally answered.

"Thanks Mom!" I shouted as I ran and hugged her around the legs. Then I turned and tossed a, "Thanks Dad," over my shoulder to Ed as I ran down the hallway to get my stuff together.

My mom found me in my room packing. "What do you have in your bag?" she asked.

"Mrs. Beasley, my pjs, and some socks," I said back, as if it were obvious that is what I would need for a weekend away from home.

"Well, that's a good start, but we might want to add some panties, some clean pants, and some clean shirts too. You go get your toothbrush and your hairbrush, and I'll get the rest of your clothes in your bag."

"Okey doke," I sang back.

As we were leaving, my mom instructed Mark and Mandy to keep an eye on me and make sure I behaved myself. I was happily tucked under Ed's arm waiting to go to the car with my Mrs. Beasley doll in hand.

When we arrived at Ed and Pat's house, she was pretty surprised to see me and said so. "What is *she* doing here?"

Ed tried to smooth it over with, "She asked if she could come, and I said yes. One more can't hurt."

"Yeah, well, you do the extra cooking and cleaning then," she retorted. "Now let's get washed up. I have dinner ready."

"What's for dinner?" Mark asked

"Liver and onions, Brussel sprouts, and rice," she said, staring Mandy in the eye. "And don't forget, you'll clean your plate, or I'll serve it to you for the next meal. We don't waste food in this house."

"Great!" Mark exclaimed. "I love liver and onions. It's one of my favorites."

Once we all washed our hands and sat down, Pat served us the portions she felt we should eat. It smelled like the green stuff floating on top of the swamp behind our house in the wintertime. I took one bite and knew I hated it. I looked at Mark for help, but he was halfway done with his and grinning between bites. Mandy was no help either. A defiant look on her face, she was sitting back in her chair, arms folded. I didn't want to cause trouble on my first visit, but it was so awful. Thinking I could make some progress with the rice and Brussel sprouts, I took a lot of bites of those before attempting the liver again. I don't know if it was the smell or the taste, but it reminded me of throw up, which gave me a brilliant idea. I had a very handy talent of throwing up at will — no finger in my throat or nothing. So, without so much as a gag for a warning, I threw up all over my plate and looked up at Pat apologetically.

"I'm sorry I threw up, Pat. I guess my tummy is all fulled up," I offered by way of explanation.

"That's fine, Sydney. Just go wash up your face. You can be excused," she said tersely as she removed my plate.

"I'll go help her," Mandy offered quickly.

"That's fine, Miranda," Pat instructed, "but I'll be saving your plate for you for breakfast." And she smiled sarcastically.

"Can I have it?" Mark asked trying to help.

"No, Mark. If you want more, I have more in the kitchen. This is for Mandy to finish," she answered smiling.

"Oh, OK," he said with an apologetic look toward Mandy as we walked down the hall to the bathroom.

When we were safely in the bathroom with the door closed, Mandy said, "I can't stand her. She's so mean. I wish I could throw up like you can."

"Want me to throw up on your plate tomorrow?" I offered.

"Yeah, but she'll know you did it on purpose. Don't worry about it. I brought some snacks, so I'll be all right."

After everyone else finished dinner, we went outside to play kick the can, even though it was already dark. Mark let me hide with him so I wouldn't be scared. Plus, I didn't really know how to play since it was my first time. We never got to the can first, but it was so much fun. Finally, Ed called out, "OK, everyone in. It's getting late." We all ran to him at the can. "Before bed," he teased, "who wants a popsicle?" All of us clamored around him shouting that we did all the way into the house.

"What's that racket all about?" Pat yelled from the kitchen as we entered.

"I told the kids they could have popsicles," Dad answered.

"Only kids who ate their dinner get popsicles," Pat said loud enough to be heard over all of us. Instantly, Mandy and I stopped clamoring and shrank back. Ed looked at us sympathetically, but just shrugged his shoulders.

"It's OK," Mandy said, "I can have a popsicle at my house anytime I want."

"No we can't," I corrected, but she just glared at me.

Pat came out of the kitchen with a box of popsicles and said, "Mark, you get to choose first," staring Anna, Bud, and Robby down, "because you are a guest, after all."

He looked at Mandy and me standing back and said, "No thank you. I think I'll pass after all."

She looked at him, then at us, and snarled like our neighbor's dog when we walked by their fence, "Fine, be that way, more for my kids then."

As Bud was opening his orange popsicle, he asked Ed, "Well, are you gonna tell them or not?"

"Damnit, Bud," Ed said with a smack on the side of his head that made him break the top of his popsicle off. It fell on the carpet.

"What the hell did you do that for?" Pat yelled.

"He knew better than to say that," Ed growled back at her. But she didn't seem to care that she was yelling at him. He just kept at Bud. "Go get a wash rag and clean that up." Bud just shrugged at Robby and Anna, as he moped to the kitchen.

"Tell us what?" Mandy finally asked.

"Well, I was gonna tell you on Sunday, but now that stupid over there opened his fat mouth, I may as well go ahead." Bud just kept scrubbing the carpet. "Now that the Kingdome construction is done, I'm gonna start working on the Alaska Pipeline, so we're moving to Anchorage," Ed stated matter-of-factly. But he was only looking at Pat, not at Mark or Mandy.

"Who is we?" Mandy asked.

"Our family," Pat answered sarcastically and waving her arm toward Anna, Bud, and Robby. Ed just gave her a dirty look.

"Will we ever get to see you?" Mark asked.

"Of course," he lied. "I'll come visit, and once we get settled, you guys can come visit us."

"But how often will you come visit?" Mark asked. His voice was thick, sounding like he was about to cry.

"I don't know, buddy, but as often as I can," Ed said ruffling his hair.

Mark just looked at orange on the carpet.

"When do you leave?" Mandy asked. She sounded mad.

"We leave next month," Pat chimed in.

"Oh," was all Mandy could muster.

And then everyone was silent. All we could hear was the sound of Bud scrubbing the carpet and the bullfrogs outside.

Finally, I blurted out, "I'm real sorry I threw up. If you

stay, I promise I won't do it ever again. I can even eat it back for breakfast if you want."

Everyone stared at me for a second before Bud and Rob started laughing. Robby said, "That's disgusting. You're so gross. Only dogs eat their puke."

"Shut up, Rob," Mark demanded with a fierce glare. Which instantly quelled their mocking.

"That'll be just about enough of that," Pat insisted in her mad voice.

"Why don't everyone just settle down here? It's time for bed anyway," Ed said standing up to let everyone know the discussion was over.

Laying in our sleeping bags on Anna's floor, I turned and whispered, "I'm real sorry Dad is leaving, Mandy," but she just rolled over so her back was facing me.

As we pulled into our driveway Sunday afternoon, I looked up at Ed and said, "Will we get to visit again before you leave?"

Smiling down at me, he said, "In two weeks, Syd."

"Great! Me and Mrs. B. will be ready."

"Mrs. B. and I," he corrected, but I didn't pay him any mind. I was just glad we'd get to go to his house one more time.

"Did you guys hear that?" I asked turning to Mark and Mandy. "We get to visit one more time before Dad moves."

Mark just got out and went in the house while we got the bags out of the trunk. Mandy said, "Yeah, that's great, Syd." But it didn't sound like she thought it was great. When we got to the front door, Mom was standing there with her hands on her hips and a worried look on her face.

"What happened? Mark didn't say a word when he came

in and then went straight to his room," she said in her just about to be mad voice.

"I threw up on my dinner and I think it made Pat mad," I offered. She looked from me to Dad knowing that was probably not what was wrong with Mark. Mandy just pushed past her and went up the stairs to her room too, leaving me standing between them.

"Syd, why don't you go put your bag away?" Mom said, not looking at me, but staring at Dad the whole time.

"Okey doke, thanks Dad," I said with a hug around his leg before leaving. "See ya in two weeks."

"See ya, Syd. See ya in two weeks," he said back with a little pat on my head.

As I headed up the stairs, I heard Mom ask, "What's going on with Mark and Mandy?" So I stopped just around the corner of the hallway to listen.

"Well, we told them that we're moving to Anchorage in a month, and they took it pretty hard."

"What, in a month? Why?" she asked. She sounded mad.

"I haven't been able to find work since the Kingdome construction finished up, and with the Boeing lay-offs, there just isn't any work around here," he said sounding kinda sad.

"Well, what are you gonna do in Anchorage?"

"Work on the pipeline they're building up there. Should be good work for a long time."

"Oh, so this is a long-term situation?" Now she was practically yelling.

"It's lookin' that way." He was hard to hear.

"Great. No wonder they're upset. Do you think you coulda given me a head's up?"

"No! I shoulda been the one to tell them, not you." Now

he sounded mad.

"Fine, you told them. Goodbye."

He slammed the door when he left.

I had to scramble to get down the hallway to my room fast because she was coming up the stairs real quick. I jumped on my bed and climbed up on the pillows to watch him get in his car and drive away, and I could hear dishes clanging around in the kitchen, so I decided to stay in my room for a while.

Chapter Five

As the bus rumbled across Oregon, I started to get cold. I fished through my bag, but I was expecting warm, California weather, so I only had one sweatshirt to try and make a blanket. Still racking my brain for how I could have come to be so fully convinced Ed was my dad and missed any clue that he wasn't, I was convinced the trip to visit him for a month had to be full of them. Then, it dawned on me, why would she even send me all the way to Alaska for an entire month when he wasn't even my dad. There's no way she could have expected them to be the least bit kind to me. I was beginning to wonder if this was my charade or hers. It didn't make any sense that she put his name on my birth certificate in the first place. Then, five years later, I just decide he's my dad and everyone goes along with it. That seems pretty convenient for her. Me having his last name and thinking Ed's my dad seems more in her best interest than mine. This way, no one's the wiser about her affair and whole mess. This way, she's just a single mom with three kids who got divorced. Sure, it's not great, but it's a hell of a lot better than married but separated and then pregnant with a married man's child. If you ask me, this narrative works out much better for her, not for me. And for Gus. He didn't even care enough to give me his name. Probably didn't want me messing up his neat little life with his other kids. I just can't for the life of me figure out why Ed and Pat would go along with it. Someone must have messed up during that month we were in Alaska. A month is a long time. I went back over that month from the beginning.

When I opened my eyes the morning we were leaving, I instantly started my three-point check system: look at the sky out my window to see if it was blue; look at the time to see if it was late enough for me to get up; and then take a few seconds to see if the miniature people who I was convinced lived under my bed and were trying to kill me every night, had succeeded in cutting off any of my body parts while I slept. I knew it was going to be a great day (it was my ninth birthday, after all): blue sky, seven forty-five so I could get up, and it appeared they had done no damage. Sitting up, I saw there was a box on the foot of my bed. I quickly climbed out from under my faded red bedspread and down to perch beside it. Uncomfortably uneven trying to sit with all my discarded stuffed animals under me, I shifted my weight to push them off onto the floor as I examined the box. There was no card, but I recognized the Shawn Cassidy wrapping paper, as the same my mom used for the white salt water sandals she gave me at the party we had with my friends the week before, so I knew it was from her. As I picked it up, the first thing I noticed was that it was very light, so I gave it a little shake and heard a faint rustle inside the box. Humph, I thought, a little disappointed — clothes of some kind. I guessed you didn't get toys anymore when you were nine. I also guessed it was something for me to either wear on our plane ride or pack for the trip. I wasn't sure if I was supposed to open it by myself or not because I'd never had a gift left on my bed before, so the rules for this sort of thing were not clear to me. By then, I had to pee really bad, so I picked up the box and leapt off my bed, careful not to step too close to the edge to be safe from the miniature people. Of course, they could not survive out from under my bed, so as long as I never got too close to the edge, I would be safe. John never believed me and just said I made them up so I could jump around all the time, but he was just mean that way. As I opened my door, package in hand my mom was coming out of her room directly across the hall.

"Why didn't you open it?" she asked, a little disappointed.

"I didn't know if it was OK or not."

"Well, of course it is. It's your birthday, after all."

"OK, but can I go potty first?"

"Of course. Here, why don't I hold it for you while you go?"

By the time I came out of the bathroom, my mom had gathered my brother and sister in the kitchen so they could watch me open my gift. I stood between their chairs and tore straight through Shawn Cassidy's face, evoking a moan of distress from my sister.

"Sorry about that," I quipped.

"I don't know how you can be so careless with such perfection," she lamented.

"It's too early for this, I'm going to be sick," Mark muttered as held his head in his hands.

I gasped as I pulled the soft pink sundress out of the box and held it up to myself. "I love it so much. Thank you, thank you, thank you," I chanted as I threw my arms around my mom's neck.

"You're welcome. I thought you'd like it."

"Oh, it's perfect. I do. Yes, I do. Thank you. I'll go get dressed. I can wear it on the plane. It'll be perfect!" I exclaimed all at once.

"It's a little early for that, isn't it?" Mark said. "We don't have to leave for the airport until two thirty and it's only like eight in the morning."

"Why don't you eat first so you don't spill on it, then take your shower and brush your teeth, then you can put it on," Mom said, sounding relieved to have come up with an excuse.

"Sounds great. What's for breakfast?" My enthusiasm was clearly annoying my siblings. It would be easy to blame it on them being teenagers with Mark fourteen and Mandy about to turn twelve, which isn't technically a teenager, but she called herself a pre-teenager. But that wasn't it. They were always grumpy in the morning, and they never appreciated my cheery disposition from the moment my eyes opened.

"What would you like? It's your birthday," my mom asked, already moving toward the sink.

I looked at my brother and sister for suggestions. Mandy mouthed the word pancakes and Mark just shrugged. "Pancakes it is," I shouted.

Breakfast was spent planning the day. Mom had to finish the last load of laundry before we could pack our suitcases, so in the meantime, each of us were supposed to shower, get dressed, and clean our rooms, real good! For me, that meant I was going to need Mandy's help, which she graciously supplied. When we were done, we all congregated downstairs in front of the laundry shrine where all clean clothes were taken from the dryer and thrown haphazardly onto an old brown couch to be dug through several times every day, most vigorously when matching socks were a necessity. Packing was one of the few times, second to company coming over, that the entire pile had to be folded. This project was often assigned to one, maybe two of us, but this time, all four of us, including Mom, were there. My mom was absently chatting away, Mark was focused and quiet, Mandy was irritated at the chaos, and I was not really helping at all, but making a good show of it by moving socks around to try and find their mates so as not to get into trouble. When the task was finally complete, we each took our piles of clean clothes up to our rooms to put them away, which to be honest, was a bit baffling to me because when you only do that every few months, who knows where things actually go?

I was in my room, pulling open drawer after drawer trying to figure out where I thought things went, when my mom went by with a suitcase for Mandy. "Hey Mom, where's my suitcase?" I yelled.

"Ah, I'll find you one. Give me a minute," she said.

Why didn't she have a suitcase for me?

Eventually, she came in with my suitcase, which she opened and put in the middle of my bed. "Here you go; I'll be back to check over what you pack to make sure you have everything you need."

"Can you please put that on the floor?"

"Wh…" She only got half her word out before she remembered the tiny people under my bed, and put it on the floor in the middle of my room so I wouldn't have to stand too close to the edge of my bed to pack.

"Thanks," I replied happily and went back to my clothes.

I don't even think I had been all the way inside the airport before. We had gone to pick up my aunt from California a few times, but we never went all the way in, only to the baggage claim. Although I knew I was excited, the car ride was eerily quiet. No one said a word. I couldn't figure out why everyone was so uptight. I, for one, was super excited!

We got there a few hours before our plane actually left.

We wanted to buy a soda, but didn't know how expensive they were, so we just sat at the windows as big as our front door and the entry window above put together, and watched huge jets take off and land one after another. They were so loud the windows would shake, yet they looked so graceful, almost like they were on a string being pulled by a huge hand. I was trying to be grown up and not act silly. It was hard, but I sat in my chair and didn't talk loud. I kept my hands folded as often as I could remember, but waving at the people leaving was too tempting. My mom finally moved over to sit on the other side of Mark and whispered something to him. He nodded and then asked me if I wanted to go watch the planes by the window. Mark was showing me the different names of the airlines. I didn't understand why we weren't flying on an Alaska airplane if we were going to Alaska. He couldn't explain it to me. He finally gave up and said we just weren't, but he hadn't lost his patience with me. He never did.

While Mark and I were lost in the thrill of the day, Mandy was terrified. She didn't want to go. The airplane scared her. The idea of going so far away scared her. What if there were bears by their house that would eat her? What if Pat was mean to her, again? What if Anna, Pat's sixteen-year-old daughter, was mean to her, again? Tears would just roll down her cheeks. My mom just hugged her and reassured her it would be all right, but I could tell something was wrong with my mom. She usually wouldn't let Mandy carry on for so long. Mark told her he'd be sure to stick up for her if anybody was mean to her. I told her I'd be her friend the whole trip so she wasn't lonely.

Finally, people showed up at the booth by our door and started shuffling papers around. As soon as they got there, my mom signaled to Mark with a nod and a look, and he took me back to the windows.

After about ten more minutes of waiting, a tall blond woman, who I thought looked like Farah Faucet on Charley's Angels, picked up the speaker that looked like John's CB radio and announced, "We will begin pre-boarding for flight 822 to Anchorage shortly. Anyone traveling with small children or who needs assistance boarding may board at this time."

My mom picked up her purse and said, "Come on, you guys, they let kids traveling alone on first, so gather up your stuff."

"Really, we get to go first?" I was so amazed! As I turned to look at the beautiful blond woman to see if she agreed, she had overheard me and was smiling. When I caught her eye, she nodded to me, and I grabbed my Mrs. Beasley doll, my bag of books, and went straight to her. It wasn't until I got there and turned around that I realized my family was still at the chairs consoling Mandy. I didn't know what to do. I looked up at her and then back at them several times and she said, "Let's see if we can't help out."

She picked up some small packages off the counter and started walking over to Mandy. "Hi, my name is Rochelle. I've got something for you. We always give these out to kids flying for the first time." She handed each of us a pin of pilot's wings. I quickly set about putting them on the strap of my pink dress, Mark slipped his in his pocket, and Mandy smiled and thanked her quietly. "A lot of people feel a bit nervous, but we will take very good care of you, I promise." She held her hand out to Mandy and waited to see if she would take it. Slowly, Mandy slipped her hand into Rochelle's, and we made our way to the open door. When we got to the door, we all stopped so we could hug and kiss mom goodbye.

"You all be very good while you're gone. You hear?" We nodded. "And you can call me anytime, you know that, but I want you to have fun. It's going to be great." As she was talking, she took each one of our chins in her hand and shook our faces a little like moms do to make sure you're paying attention. "I love you." And then, she nodded to Rochelle, who turned and walked us down the tunnel, Mandy still with tears rolling down her cheeks, but she went. I, on the other hand skipped under my mother's glare, who was always telling me to walk, not hippity-hop everywhere I went. At the doorway to the plane, Rochelle introduced us to the stewardess, Amanda who showed us the cockpit right inside the door. The pilot and co-pilot were already seated and going through checklists, but they each greeted us for a moment. The cockpit was amazing to my nine-year-old eyes. I thought the pilots to be the smartest people I'd ever seen to know what all the buttons were for. We had a window seat and an aisle seat side by side, but Mark was sitting by himself a few rows behind Mandy and me. I guessed that is what my mom was talking to him about for so long after she talked to the blond Farah Faucet lady.

By the time we left the cockpit, Mandy had stopped crying and was acting much more like herself, taking care of me. She sat by the window to start with because I didn't want to.

We were the first to get off the plane. Amanda helped us get our stuff and walked us to the end of the ramp. I saw them standing at the end of the tunnel, and I took off running. I jumped into Ed's arms, *not noticing their surprise to see me.* I was thrilled to be there. I even hugged Pat and Anna, who stiffly endured my affection. Next, I turned to my stepbrothers, Bud and Rob, grinning, but they backed away with grimaces on their faces. Undaunted by their rebuff, I tucked myself under Dad's arm after he hugged Mark and Mandy as he announced there were some cool things to see in the airport. After we walked all around the Anchorage Airport and saw the stuffed moose that was taller at its chin than Dad, the Kodiak bear, the salmon and crab that were bigger than my bed at home, and the rat sized mosquitoes — all stuffed and in display cases — we were headed to a surprise. I was sure it was for me, being that it was my birthday after all.

When we got home, there were more than a few surprises. The first one was that they didn't live in a house at all, but an old, singlewide trailer in a park with lots of old singlewide trailers. It was made from dirty white corrugated metal on the outside. There were three rickety steps up to the brown front door that opened to a brown paneled living room and kitchen. There was no yard to play in, but some patchy grass out between the driveways. It was so tiny that all eight of us couldn't be in the kitchen or living room at the same time. The hallway was so skinny, I felt like we were walking through a maze. The girls were going to share Anna's room. She had bunk beds on one side of the room and there was just enough space between the bed and the wall for me to lie on the floor in my sleeping bag each night. Instantly, I was very concerned because I would be right by the little people under her bed and they would for sure get me, but Mark assured me it never gets dark there, so they couldn't come out. There wasn't enough room for more than one person to be standing up at a time. We had to take turns sitting on the bed until each person was dressed and out. At the end of the bed was a closet the size of our refrigerator at home, and that was it.

Our second surprise was a party. There were crape paper streamers decorating the kitchen and the living room with balloons taped in bunches in the corners. There was a cake and a present on the kitchen counter. I couldn't believe my eyes. It was better than the slumber party I had with my friends before we left. The thought that all this wasn't for me, never crossed my mind until I looked closely at the cake, and even then, it didn't register.

"There are too many candles on this cake. I'm only nine," I said confused.

"Oh sweetie, that cake isn't for you, it's for your brother. We didn't get to see him for his birthday last week, you know." I hated it when Pat tried to sound soft. There wasn't a soft part of her, and I knew it even then, but my disbelief got the best of me.

"But didn't you know, it's my birthday today?" I asked, genuinely confused.

"Yeah, we know, but this party is for Mark, we were only expecting him, you know."

"Oh, I know," I said indignantly. I looked right into Pat's black eyes as round as olives and said, "The nice thing about my brother is that he shares with me." I walked away from her and straight to Mandy.

I thought I was hiding how badly I felt, but Mandy knew right away. I like to think it is because she knew me so well that she could tell, but I think it was obvious and Pat had the satisfaction of knowing that she had gotten me.

"Excuse me, everyone, I think we need to lay some ground rules. There are so many of us, we need to understand how things are going to work if you're going to be here soooo long. First of all, you don't call me Pat, you call me Mom. Second of all, Mark and Sydney sleep on the floors, the others sleep on the beds. You clean up your own messes, you eat all the food you're given, and if you talk back to me, I will put cayenne pepper on your tongue. Is that clear? Good, now let's get on with the party. Mark, would you like to open your gift first, or have cake and ice cream first?"

"I'm pretty hungry, maybe we could eat first."

"Great, you just sit down and open your gift, and then we'll cut the cake."

"OK," confusion clear in his tone as he glanced at Mandy and me.

By this time, Mandy was fuming. She was not going to let this go so she said very loud and very deliberately, "Pat, I thought he said he wanted to eat first. Why give him the choice if you're going to do it your way anyway?"

"Well, because at least that way you get to guess what I want and try to do it my way on your own. It'll be good practice for you if you want to get along in this house." Her forced laugh convinced no one. She had not spoken in jest, but earnest. "And that, young lady, is borderline talking back. Watch it, or you'll get cayenne pepper."

She handed Mark his gift. He slowly opened it, not knowing what else to do. His blue eyes grew round as he stared at the Instamatic Polaroid camera in his lap.

"Wow, this is so cool, thanks Dad. These are the newest thing going."

"Yeah, I know, they're so cool. The picture comes out right away and you can see it."

"Here, let me help you load the film, and then you can give it a try."

As we all watched Dad load the film, Mark caught my eye.

"Here you go, Syd, you take the first picture. Here, take

59

one of me and Dad."

"Wait just a second, let me get in there," Pat insisted as she squeezed between them on the couch.

So I took the first picture of Mark, Pat, and Dad sitting on the couch, Pat in the middle. The flash went off first, and the zshzshzsh noise the film made as it slid out the front of the camera amazed me. Mark held it under his arm until it was beginning to develop. He was the first to get a glimpse of the images appearing and quickly put it in the box the camera came in. He saw that I had only taken a picture of him, cutting Pat and Dad out.

"Why are you putting it in the box? Let us see the picture," Pat insisted.

"That one didn't turn out, we'll have to try again." Mark looked a warning at me, and I knew it had turned out just fine.

Ten days went by, and it was Mandy's birthday. On the morning of July 10th, Pat came singing into our doorway. She couldn't come into the room, of course; I was sleeping on the floor. I had found a way to come to terms with the miniature people under Anna's bed that I was way too close to. After a few nights, I believed what Mark said that first night about it never really getting dark at night there, so they wouldn't dare try and hurt me. I was also unable to perform my three-point check system each morning because Anna had to close her blinds every night because it was so light out, and I couldn't see the clock from the floor, so each morning I just had to decide it was all OK and go with it. I'm surprised she didn't step right on me, but for some reason, she didn't. She just stood in the door and sang Happy Birthday to Mandy. She was turning twelve, a pre-teenager as she had told me a hundred times for the past month! Anybody else would have thought

Pat was going out of her way to be nice to Mandy, but we knew better — if she was being nice, she either wanted something in return, or she wanted to make someone else feel bad. That someone else was me again. She made a big breakfast of orange French toast and bacon that we ate in shifts of three at a time. We all got dressed up, which really meant we wore shoes, and went to the mall. Nobody knew what was up except for Pat, and it was tempting to be excited. She led us to a real jewelry store and told Mandy, "You, young lady, may pick out some ruby earrings, for we are going to get your ears pierced today," in her sappy sweet voice that really made you want to throw up, which I was tempted to do right there, just for the effect.

Later that night, after we had cake, we were all crammed into the living room and half in the kitchen for stories. Being the smallest, I was sitting on the floor between the couch and the chair in the living room, between Ed and Pat. Mark and Mandy were on the couch with Ed. Pat decided we should all hear how we were born in honor of the birthday celebration. Ed started with Mark.

"Oh man, when you were born, I don't think I had ever been that excited before. We were still living in Everett and your mom was huge. Well, you were huge, so she had to be, right? Finally, one night she nudged me and said, 'Ed, I think it's time'. We had a bag packed and were excited to finally be going to the hospital. We called my mom and Ethel to tell them we were going. They said they'd meet us there. We drove up to Providence, and they took your mom into the labor room. I had to wait in the hall or the waiting room. And wait did I. It took a long time, many hours before they took your mom down to the delivery room where there was another waiting room for

61

all of us. Of course, I didn't know what was going on inside the room because they wouldn't let me in there, but I could hear a lot of screaming and hurried voices, and I was worried. Finally, we heard a cry. It must have been an hour before the doctor came out and told me I had a son. I don't think I could have grinned any bigger with the face God gave me. 'But', the doctor said, 'the delivery was very hard on Leslie. The baby was so big that he got stuck and we had to give her the choice of breaking his collarbone or of pushing him back up the birth canal and pulling his arms over his head so he would fit. She chose the latter to save her baby the pain, and she is in bad shape for it. We think she'll recover, but she'll have to go to intensive care for a day or so. You'll be able to see her there'.

'What about my son, is he all right? Can I see him too?'

'Yes, your son is fine. He weighs ten pounds eight ounces and is very strong. He is on his way to the nursery and you can see him after they get him bathed, fed, and wrapped'.

"Well, I was so excited I started handing out the cigars I had bought for just this occasion when I was stationed in Cuba. Oh, you'll get a kick out of this knowing your mother. Just then, they wheeled her out of the delivery room to take her to intensive care. She looked so white she could have been dead. But she got up on one elbow and said to my mother, 'Did you see my skinny, anemic baby?'. And was right back down on her back again. You see my mother had been telling her that because she didn't drink any milk or eat any green vegetables while she was pregnant, she was going to have a skinny, anemic baby. We laughed about that for a long time."

"What about me, what about me?" Mandy coaxed.

"OK, OK, you were a different story all together, Miranda Michele."

"Your mom and I weren't doing very well then, but she wanted me to come into the delivery room this time. The doctors were letting people do that by then, and she wasn't too nervous having been through it once. So when it was time for you to be born, she called me, and I rushed over and took her to the hospital. Again, it took a while, but then it was time, and I got to see you come out. You were all pink and purple and screaming, like you'd been spanked with a belt before anyone even touched you. The doctor held you up for a brief moment before the nurses took over. You were the most beautiful sight I'd ever seen, so raw and untainted in your first moments of life. I couldn't get the Cubans that time, but I had cigars for all the family, and we celebrated. It wasn't so hard on your mom this time, so she could go home in only a few days."

I was watching my sister. There was pride and overwhelming joy on her face as she basked in her father's rare love.

"Mark was so excited to have a baby sister. We named you after Miranda, who was our best friend back in Rhode Island when I was still in the service."

"My turn, what about me, Dad?" I interrupted him. More than the story, I wanted to hear how cherished I was. It had not registered to me that he said he and my mom were already separated before Mandy was born —

"You, well Sydney, I didn't even know you were born for a few weeks. That's the way it goes sometimes, you know. Can't say as I cared much either." The room froze and everyone gaped at me, wondering what I'd do. I could feel their eyes on me as I tried with everything I had not to let the tears welling in my eyes and throat betray the severity of the wound he'd inflicted upon me. I don't ever remember being so determined not to cry. I focused fiercely on one strand of the brown shag carpet until my brother finally came to my rescue.

"Wow, I'm pretty tired, I think I'll hit it."

With that, everyone began to move, clearing dishes and negotiating shifts in the bathroom.

Somehow, I escaped Pat's watchful eye and skipped my turn through their room to brush my teeth. I probably should have peed, but I'd rather take my chances outside with a bear than face her or dad that night. I sat curled up in a ball in my Minnie Mouse nightie by the closet until Anna and Mandy were in bed so I could roll out my sleeping bag and crawl in. When I was sure they were asleep, I cried that night in my bed, but I told myself I would only give it one night of crying, but no more. Many nights I would crawl in bed with either Mandy or Mark and finally go to sleep. I tried to be brave when we talked to Mom on the phone. After that night, Alaska was no longer fun or beautiful. It was just something to survive until I got to go home. It was a few nights later that I lay there and instead of trying hard not to cry, I made up my own version of *Jesus Loves Me* to comfort myself. It went: "Jesus loves me, this I know. You may hate me, why I don't know, but Jesus loves me, this I know." I sang that over and over to myself until I fell asleep each night, for twenty-one nights, until we went home.

Chapter Six

I found tears wet on my cheeks without realizing they were there. I hadn't thought about that trip to Alaska in such a long time. I was becoming more confused as to why Ed would go along with this whole charade than I was by my inability to remember Gus was my dad. I closed my eyes and tried to go back to sleep, but sleep was as evasive as the truth. Eventually, my mind wandered back to my ninth year. What else I kept asking myself? What else? Was that the year I met Pam, started going to Awana? I think so, but what does that have to do with anything? But I wouldn't rule anything out. I just tried to remember it all.

My eyes opened in a burst, like they did every morning. First, I looked up to see the sky out my window. It was pretty cloudy, with only a little bit of blue way far away. "Doesn't look good, Mrs. Beasley," I said out loud. Then, I rolled over to check the clock behind my head on the shelf inside my headboard to see if it was too early for me to wake up, the second step in my three-point check system. "Only six fifty-six, Mrs. Beasley. We have to wait four minutes," I said, clearly irritated with the way this was going. Rolling back over, I held still to take stock of how I felt to see if the miniature people had made it out from under my bed in the night and done any damage. Nothing hurt, so at least that was OK. I picked up Mrs. Beasley to discuss the day with her. "It's Sunday, so what should I wear to church?" I waited for her reply. "No, pants are not OK for church. And those kids are nicer than the kids at school, so I don't have to worry about them teasing me about my hairy legs. What's that? Yeah, I guess it could be cold outside, so I'll wear some tights, just to be on the safe side. Besides, you never know if James is going to be there, and he's not that nice. OK, don't let me forget to take some offering money out of Mom's purse. I forgot the last two weeks, and it's embarrassing. Maybe we should take extra to make up for it? What do you think? Well, that's a little risky. If we take more than a few quarters, she might notice. Better not!" I rolled over to check the time again, and it was just turning to seven. "Well, what do ya know, time to get up. Let's get this show on the road."

I jumped as gently as I could a little way away from my bed and went to my closet to get a dress out. I decided on the green one my grandma made me. Then, I opened my top drawer and pulled out some blue tights. I thought about changing my panties, but decided it would be a hassle, and just pulled on the tights and dress. Keeping close to my dresser, I skirted over to my door, and gently pulled it open to go to the bathroom. I had to double check and make sure the secret door into my mom and John's room was closed so I didn't wake them up when I went potty and brushed my teeth. I tried to brush my long hair the best I could. When I was satisfied I looked my best, I went down the hall to the kitchen for some breakfast. I opened the bottom cupboard so I could stand on the shelf to climb on the counter to get to the top cupboard where the cereal was. Balancing on the edge of the counter, I pulled down the box of Cheerios and shut the door. Staying on top of the counter, I slid over the skinny edge in front of the sink to get a bowl out. Then I slid down on my tummy so I didn't make a loud thump when I landed on the floor. I poured the cereal into my bowl, then went to the fridge to get the milk. Once I had my milk all poured, I carefully carried the way too full bowl over to the table where the sugar shaker was and made my cereal look like a field after a good snow. I grabbed a spoon out of the drawer and ate standing up so I wouldn't spill on my dress. Really, I was only interested in the top layer, so once that was gone, I poured the rest in the garbage can, and put my bowl and spoon in the dishwasher. Then, I repeated all the gymnastics it took to get the cereal out so I could put it back. I had my coat on and was just about to close the front door when I remembered the money for my offering, so I snuck back up the stairs to find my mom's purse. She usually left it in the kitchen somewhere, but I didn't notice it when I was eating breakfast. I looked around, but didn't see it. Afraid of being late, I was just going to go without when I noticed it perched on the edge of the couch. I smiled with satisfaction and opened her wallet, unzipped the little part where she kept quarters, and took three out. Once they were safely zipped in my coat pocket and my mom's wallet was back where it went, I tiptoed back down the stairs, and went outside to wait at the end of the driveway for the Sunday School bus, like I had every week for the past four years.

I didn't have to wait long before I saw the big yellow bus coming down the street. It stopped in front of me, and Mr. Bruce opened the big doors for me to climb the three black stairs, round the corner, and sit in any of the empty green seats, for I was the only kid on the bus, again. "Good morning to you, Miss. Sydney," Mr. Bruce said, like he did every Sunday.

"Good morning right back, Mr. Bruce," I said, like I did every Sunday.

"And how are you this morning?"

"Just dandy, thanks. How are you?" We had the same conversation every week. I really liked Mr. Bruce. He had a really nice voice, and he always called me Miss. Sydney.

"Well, Miss. Sydney. I've got a bit of bad news that's making me a bit sad this morning."

"What is it?" I asked him, concerned.

"Well, you know how there are never any other kids on the bus?" he said slowly.

"Yeah, it's always just me," I said, a little nervous.

"Well, the church has decided we can't afford to have the Sunday School bus anymore because it's really expensive and with the gas shortages, and not very many people using it, well, this is the last week for the Sunday School bus," he said very sad. I thought he was going to cry.

"Oh," was all I could manage. "I know about that. My mom complains about how she has to sit in the gas line all the time. She really hates it."

"Yeah, well, I'll miss seeing you every week. I'm really sorry about it."

"I'll miss you too, Mr. Bruce." And I hung my head down and thought, see Mrs. Beasley, when the morning check system doesn't go well, it's gonna be a bad day.

We rode the rest of the way to church in silence. As Mr. Bruce opened the door for me, he said, "See you after church, Miss. Sydney," with a sad smile.

"OK, see ya. Thanks, Mr. Bruce," I said as I waved from the bottom of the stairs. And I turned and walked into Sunday School for the last time where I planned to pray for another bus.

It was the Wednesday after my last bus ride to church, and

I was still a little sad about it. I really liked Sunday School and hearing about how much Jesus loved me. And I really liked riding the bus with Mr. Bruce. I lived across the street from my elementary school, so I didn't get to ride a bus to school. I was sitting at my desk waiting for Mr. Baker, my third-grade teacher, to tell us which math groups we were in.

I was in the orange group with a bunch of kids I had never been with before, and most of them were pretty smart, so I decided I must have moved up. I sat next to a girl with crazy red hair named Pam. She was in my reading group too, and I really liked her.

"So, how do you like being an orange?" she asked me.

"Seems OK. I mean, I like oranges, and all," I said back.

"Yeah, me too, better than bananas for sure!" she said smiling.

"Hey, wanna play together at recess?" I asked.

"You bet I do," she said with a huge grin.

Mrs. Jacobson was our parent helper. She was a nice lady who helped in our class a lot, so we all knew her really well. Before we knew it, Mr. Baker sang out, "It is time, it is time, my friends… to gather up your pencils, put them away. Work before play, but now, it is time to play, play, play."

Anxious to get out on the playground, we quickly gathered up our math stuff and put it back in our own desks before lining up at the back door that led out to the field and playground. Pam was standing in front of me, and when Mr. Baker opened the door and sang us out to play, she reached back and took my hand to walk outside together. Once we were through the door, she kept a hold of my hand and we walked toward the playground, chatting about what we should do.

"What games do you like to play?" she asked.

"Well, I don't like the bars anymore," I insisted.

"Oh, I remember when you got stitches on your lip back in the beginning of the year! There was sooooo much blood all over your shirt."

"I know! And it was so hard to hold my lip still while they stuck the needle in there to make it numb. It was way worse than when I got stitches in my chin. See this scar?" I said as I lifted my chin to show her the scar from the ice-skating accident the year before.

"Wow, that's big!" she exclaimed, obviously impressed. "Have you gotten any other stitches?"

"Nope, just my chin and my lip. And I hope I never do again. The stitches don't hurt, but the needle to make the stitches not hurt is the worst! Have you ever had any stitches?"

"No, never. But I have broken my arm before."

"Really?"

"Yep. I fell at Awana last year and broke my left arm."

"What's Awana?"

"Awana is sooooo much fun. Even though I did break my arm, it's still fun. It's like church, but actually way more fun. At the beginning, you play lots of running games. That's when I broke my arm. And then you go to the lesson time where you learn a Bible story and you have a workbook where you do homework and learn a verse. It's great. Hey, it's tonight. You should come with me. All you have to do is get your mom to drive you to my house, and then there's a bus that takes us to Alderwood Junior High and then it takes everyone back home afterward."

"Really, there's a bus?" I couldn't believe there was a bus that would take me. "What time do I have to be there?" I was so excited, I could not believe my ears. It hadn't even been one

Sunday without Mr. Bruce and Sunday School, and I had another bus to take me to church. Now, I just had to get my mom to drive me to Pam's house.

"The bus comes at six thirty, and I get home about eight forty-five, so I can get in bed by nine, which is past my bedtime, but my mom says it's OK just on Wednesdays."

"OK, but where do you live?"

"I will write down my address when we get back in, OK?"

The rest of the day went by so slow. I could not wait to get home and get ready for Awana. We had to write a sentence with twelve words in it before we could go home each day, which for some kids, and for me on some days, was hard. But not that day. My sentence was, 'Jesus answered my prayer for a bus to take me to church'. When Mr. Baker finally sang us out the door, I sprinted across the street to start getting ready.

I burst in the door and took the stairs two at a time. John was in the kitchen baking peanut butter cookies.

"Hey, slow down there, Sal," he yelled as I turned the corner heading for my room.

"Can't, gotta get my homework done so I can go to Awana tonight," I tossed back over my shoulder.

"What the hell is Awana? And you're not going anywhere until your chores are done," he shouted after me.

"Dang, Mrs. Beasley," I muttered as I threw my coat and backpack on the pile of stuffed animals on the foot of my bed, "I forgot about my chores. But don't worry. I can do it. They won't take long," I reassured her frozen smiling face perched on my pillows. Wednesdays were my day to feed the rabbits, clean up the dog poop in the back yard, and take out the garbage. If Mandy actually cleaned up the poop on Monday, it wouldn't be too bad. If she didn't, then it could take a while.

"I'll be right back, Mrs. B., gotta take care of the rabbits and the dog poo," I said, pulling on my boots.

I fed the rabbits and cleaned up the poop that had been accumulating since last Wednesday. Obviously, Mark skipped Friday and Mandy skipped Monday. On my way up the back-porch steps, I thought to myself, I'm gonna remember to tell Mom it's not fair that they didn't do their job. When I got to the back door, it was locked. I pulled again to make sure, but it was locked. John was standing at the table, right inside, so I knew he locked it. I knocked, even though I knew he heard and saw me standing there trying to get in. Without ever looking my direction, he just smiled to himself and kept rolling cookie balls and placing them on cookie sheets. Exasperated, I stomped my foot on each step back down the stairs, and all the way around the house to the front door. Each stomp of my way, I muttered out loud, "I wish my mom was here, I wish my mom was here, I wish my mom was here." When I got there, I heard the lock click. I tried the knob, but it was locked.

"John, open the door!" I yelled. But I just heard foot-steps going up the stairs.

I stormed around to the back door of the garage, but it was locked too. Furious, I went back to the slider and saw him back in the kitchen, laughing to himself. Tears of frustration filled my eyes despite my best efforts to not give him the satisfaction. "John, can you please let me in?" I asked.

"Front door's open, maybe. I wish you weren't so dumb," he said without even looking at me.

After resting my head on the glass for a few seconds, I turned and made my way back around the house to the front door. Thankfully, the handle turned in my hand and I could open the door.

As soon as I opened it, he yelled, "Make sure you take those muddy boots off, young lady," in a stern voice. I didn't answer. Instead, I continued stomping in my stocking feet through the house gathering up the garbage cans to take back outside to the side of the house to be emptied. When I went to get the kitchen garbage can, he grabbed me by the arm — painfully squeezing my tiny arm in his huge hand, spun me around, pulled me so my face was almost touching his, and growled more than spoke, "When I speak to you, you will answer, do you hear me?"

"Yes," I whispered back, more scared than angry.

He held me there, really hurting my arm, for another few seconds before he shoved me back into the counter, the corner gouging my spine. I grit my teeth hard such that only a gasp escaped my mouth, but he smiled just the same. He knew it hurt me, and he was satisfied. I grabbed the bag out of the can, put a new one in, and left as quietly as I could.

When I crept back in the front door, relieved it was unlocked and I didn't have to play the game of going around to the back and front again, I leaned in the corner against the golden windows that hugged the white front door. As I shrugged off my boots and picked them up to carry them up the thread-worn green carpeted stairs, John was bent over pulling a pan of cookies out of the oven. Trying to keep my head down so as not to catch his eye, I hugged the corner at the top of the stairs to make my way down the hallway to finally get to my homework. Thinking I had made it, John's voice curled behind me like black smoke. "Hey, get that drain cleaned out. The damn tub won't drain and it's your stringy hair clogging it up. Pop that plate and pull out that nasty mess."

"Yes, sir," I mumbled with just enough volume to not earn

his ire.

"Watch that tone, young lady," he snarled but he was going back to his cookies, so I got away with my borderline sassy sir.

I was only a few steps away from the bathroom, so I stopped at the hall closet door, opened it and found the screwdriver and needle nose pliers on the shelf that held everything from batteries to q-tips. I noticed the pink and white vinyl floor was starting to pull up a little at the edge of the tub as I knelt and leaned over the edge, the rail of the shower doors digging into my ribs as I reached to unscrew the plate covering the drain. The tub was a little dirty with a brown ring starting to form about half way up the side. *This is what he's so mad about. Might not be that my hair is clogging the drain. Could be that five people shower in here every day and it just gets dirty. And we all have hair, not just me.* But I knew better to even mutter these thoughts. He'd hear me, somehow. Once I got the plate off, I dug deep into the dark tube that I imagined to be the tunnel where the little people who lived under my bed came from. I scooped the screwdriver against the side and pulled up gently, feeling the slight resistance of the hair that was always there. As soon as I scraped up against it, I smelled it — the stale, wet stink that reminded me of the swamp out behind our house on the hot summer days. I coaxed the clump up a bit, but quickly set the screwdriver down and sat back on my heels, not only to give my ribs a break from the sharp edge of the rails but to get the real tool I needed, the needle nose pliers. I reached them down into the dark tube and slowly got a hold of the dark mass. You have to pull gently so as not to break it apart. As gross as it is, there is some satisfaction in pulling it all up in one long, slimy piece. It's sort of like peeling

74

a Christmas orange in one long curl. You get one hunk out and lay it down on the lip of the hole and then grab the next piece inside, being careful to keep your head back because the tangled mess of hair and shampoo and conditioner will make you gag. I've only thrown up once, and now I know. It only takes a few minutes to get the big lump out and into the garbage can. I popped the plate back on and screwed it back in place. I thought about not cleaning the tub, but I knew better. He'd come and check, and if he was mad, I didn't have a chance to go to Awana. So I sprinkled the blue Comet all over the tub and splashed water up and down the sides before scrubbing it with the brush from under the sink. You have to use your hand to wipe it off when you splash the water back over it, otherwise it leaves a streak and that just won't do. Trust me. I wiped off the screwdriver and pliers and put them back in the closet.

With my chores done, I was back in my room wanting to take Mrs. Beasley into my closet and swear at the dog like I usually did when John was so mean, but I had to get my homework done so I would be ready to go to Awana when my mom came home. It was already four forty-five, and I still had to eat too.

When I finally got back into my room, I pulled up the back of my shirt to see the V-shaped cut and bruise forming in the middle of my back. "He's such a jerk, Mrs. B," I mumbled, "There was red hair in the clump too, not just my brown hair. Plus, Mom, Mandy, and Mark have brown hair too," as I hopped onto my bed, pulled my backpack up beside me and Mrs. B., and took out my spelling worksheet. By five thirty, I had finished my spelling, math, and read for my fifteen minutes for the night. All I had to do was get something to eat

75

so I was ready when my mom got home from picking Mandy up from her practice. I sure hoped John was done with his cookies and out of the kitchen. I put everything back in my backpack so it would be ready for school, put Mrs. B. back in her spot on my pillow, and leapt to the middle of my room. First, I cracked my door a little to see if I could hear the TV. It sounded like the news was on, which was a good sign for me because that meant John was probably in the living room. As casually as I could, I strolled down the hall and into the kitchen. Sure enough, I saw the top of John's head poking over the top of the gold rocking chair, so the coast was clear. I opened the fridge and took out all of the stuff for a sandwich, plus an apple. Just as I was opening the bread drawer, I heard John yell, "Hey, no snacks before dinner. We're going to eat as soon as your mom gets home."

"I'm not having a snack. I have Awana tonight, so I have to make a sandwich because I won't be here for dinner," I said as nice as I could.

"What the hell is Awana?" he asked for the second time since I got home from school.

"It's like church, but on Wednesdays. My friend, Pam, invited me to go with her," I answered. I didn't want to make him mad again for not answering him.

"I don't know who you think is going to drive you there. Your mom isn't gonna wanna turn around and leave again right after she just got home from work and picking up Mandy. And I'm sure as hell not driving you."

"Well, I'll ask her, just in case she might say yes," I said, hoping and believing she would. My mom would usually do almost anything to help me out.

When my mom finally did get home at six, I was sitting

on the top stair with my coat on and the piece of paper with Pam's address in my hand.

"Hi, Mom, how was your day?" I said as soon as she opened the door.

"Why do you have your coat on?" she asked suspiciously, ignoring my question.

"Well, you see. I know you don't like us to ask you questions right away when you get home, but I don't have time to wait, so I'm sorry ahead of time for asking right away. But my friend, Pam, invited me to go to Awana with her tonight. The bus picks her up at her house at six thirty. If I am there, it will take me too. Then, every Wednesday after this, it will pick me up here, and you won't have to drive me anymore. And the bus will bring me home," I gushed out eagerly. "Can I please go? I have done all of my chores, all of my homework, I ate a sandwich and an apple, and I have my stuff ready for school tomorrow."

Walking up the stairs and making her way past me, she asked, "What is Awana, where is it, and where does Pam live?"

"Awana is like church, but on Wednesdays. It's at Alderwood Junior High, you know, Mark's school."

"Yes, I know Mark's school," she said giving me a look.

"Oh, yeah. Anyway, here is Pam's address. She said she doesn't live very far away." My mom took the paper and looked at the address. I could tell she was thinking. "Remember, Sunday when Mr. Bruce said that was the last day they would have the Sunday School bus? Well, I asked Jesus to send me a new bus, and he did."

With that, Mark, who had been sitting in the living room listening said, "It's hard to argue with God, Ma," and chuckled to himself.

77

Just then John piped in, "I think this is ridiculous. It's dinnertime and you just got home. These kids don't need to be hauled all over creation all the time."

Afraid I was losing momentum, I sat down in the kitchen chair and started to take my coat off when my mom asked me, "What time does the bus bring you back home?"

My head popped back up, and I answered quickly, "By eight forty-five so I can be in bed by nine. I know it's a little past my bedtime, but it's just on Wednesdays."

"OK, well let's get going. We don't want to miss that bus, now do we?" my mom said smiling. "I'll be back in about twenty minutes, and then we'll eat," she announced to everyone else.

I jumped up, put my coat back on and bounded down the stairs. Just as I was leaving the house, I heard John complaining, "These damn kids are so spoiled."

When I was lying in my bed that night telling Mrs. B. all about my first night at Awana, I couldn't decide which was the best part: the bus, the games, or that I had my own workbook with actual Bible verses to memorize. I decided I liked the fact that I was in the Chums. Mrs. B. and I just liked the sound of it. It was just a simple prayer for help getting to church.

Chapter Seven

Finding these memories much easier to navigate, I stuck with this ninth year. It seemed I was old enough by then to really be able to remember things clearly. Maybe if I foraged through everything I could access, something would make more sense. Someone had to have slipped up somewhere along the way. The night sky was bright with the stars that gave the hope of a cloudless day to follow. I smiled to think of my silly check point system when I was little. If only blue skies in the morning really meant all was right in the world.

"Hey Ma," Mark called through the house as he bound up the stairs two at a time. "Ma? Moooom." I put down my Box Car Children book, jumped off the foot of my bed, and opened my door to see what the excitement was about. He sounded like something great was up by the tone of his voice, and I never liked to miss out on anything.

"I'm going to the bathroom," she replied.

"Hey Mom," he asked, as he pushed open the bathroom door with Mandy and me standing behind him to see what was so exciting. Of course, the door was not locked. With only one bathroom and five people, there was a strict rule about not ever, for any reason, locking the bathroom door. No matter what you were doing in there, you had to share the room. Unphased by the three of us standing in the doorway, she looked up from her book to see what Mark wanted. "Can you take me and Bobby ice skating Friday night? There will be a bunch of other kids there."

"What time?" she asked back, showing good signs of saying yes.

"The open skate is from seven till ten, and with my ASB card, it only costs two dollars."

"Sure, why not," she said agreeably.

"Can we come?" Mandy chimed in.

"Of course."

"Sweet!" Mark said as he pumped his fist.

"Now, can you guys go back out and close the door?" my mom requested as she returned to her book.

"Mandy, do you know how to ice skate?" I asked following her back down the hallway to her room.

"No, but it can't be much harder than roller skating, and we know how to do that." She sounded confident enough, so I thought it'd be fun.

I jumped back on my bed to tell Mrs. Beasley that I was going ice-skating in just two days. She was very impressed!

When Friday night finally came, I wore my white jeans, a white turtle-neck, my pink sweatshirt, with my multi-colored ski hat and scarf that my mom crocheted for me on her wooden loom. The ice rink was in Edmonds, just one town away from where we lived. I felt a little nervous about not knowing how, but I kept remembering what Mandy said about knowing how to roller skate. After my mom paid for each of us, we went to get skates that fit. They had little cubbies full of skates that went from the floor all the way to the ceiling on three walls of a room the size of our living room at home. My mom told the guy I wore a size thirteen.

"Just sit right here, and I will lace them up for you and make sure they fit right." The guy with the skates looked nice enough, so after a nervous glance at my mom who smiled and nodded, I sat down on the red carpeted bench and held out my foot. "Have you ever ice skated before?" he asked while lacing up my first skate.

"No, but I know how to roller skate," I offered.

"That's great," he said glancing up from my laces to smile reassuringly. "You'll do just fine."

"She has also been snow skiing, since she was two," my mom said.

"Oh well, in that case, you'll have no problem at all. You already know what a slippery surface feels like," he said looking up to smile at me again as he laced up my second skate. "Just be real careful of the brakes here on the toe. If you go up on the toe of the skates, you'll stop real quick, so be careful about that. Otherwise, I bet you pick it up in half a lap around the rink. But be careful walking down the stairs. They're not so good to walk in."

"Thanks," I said shyly.

Man, was he right. Walking was so wobbly. My ankles felt like they were pieces of cooked spaghetti, so my mom held me under my armpits and helped me down the stairs and to the edge of the ice. Mark and Mandy were already going around the rink pretty quickly. I let go of my mom to cling to the wall, and slowly groped my way along, slipping and nearly falling with every motion of my legs. But he was right, in just a little bit, I could slide one foot and then the next foot and only hold the wall just in case. By the time I was half way around the rink, opposite where my mom was sitting and watching intently, I had let go of the wall completely, and was sort of skating by myself. But then, I wobbled and lurched, and in my flailing to recover, went forward on the brakes. Before I knew what happened, I was face down on the ice with my arms flung out to each side. It happened so fast, I did not get my hands in front of me at all, and I landed chin first. Stunned by the fall, it took several seconds for the pain in my chin to hit me. I could hear my mom yelling at Mark to get me, but I wasn't sure what he was supposed to get me for yet. Then, the pain started to kick in, and it felt like my chin was being crushed with a pair of pliers. It wasn't until I saw the blood seeping into the ice around me that I started to panic and cry. By the time Mark got to me and rolled me over to a sitting position, the blood on the ice was the size of a basketball. But when he sat me up, the gash on my chin started gushing blood all over my white jeans and light pink sweatshirt, and I thought I was going to bleed to death. I tried to put my hand on my chin, but Mark held it back. The flesh was hanging open along the entire length of my chin and he didn't want me to touch it. Sitting on the ice crying and in shock from the blood pouring on my chest and lap, I scanned for my mom. There were too many people gathered around for me to see her, and before I knew it, someone had picked me up in his arms and was skating with me to the edge of the ice where my mom was waiting. He effortlessly moved from skating to running up the stairs with my mom right behind him and laid me on a table. Finally, I could see her as she took my hand and rubbed my forehead saying, "You're going to be fine. It's just a cut on your chin. They bleed a lot, but it's not that bad, honey."

Then the man was back with a white bandage that he put over my chin and he started pushing on it, which made me scream out in pain. Instantly, my mom's reassuring eyes darted from my face to his. "What are you doing to her?" she demanded.

"That cut needs pressure on it," he answered back matter-of-factly. All the while, he continued working. He held the bandage there while taping it in place super tight by wrapping a bandage around my entire head.

My mom gave up glaring at him and returned to reassuring me. "Just hang in there. He's helping you. This will slow down the bleeding. You're doing great."

"OK, that will hold her until you get her to the hospital. She's gonna need some stitches. But you're only five minutes away, so you should be fine." With that, he sat me up slowly, scooped me back in his arms, and said, "Lead the way, I'll get her to your car for you."

On the way back through the lobby, my mom said to Mark, "You guys stay here and skate. I'm going to take Syd to the hospital for some stitches, and we'll be back before the session is over. She'll be fine." Without giving him a chance to answer, she was holding the door open for him to carry me out into the chilly October air.

My mom parked close, and carried me, just like the man at the ice rink had, into the emergency room doors. I don't know if the emergency room was slow that night, or if me being completely covered in blood with my entire head wrapped in gauze and tape when we arrived is what made it go so fast, but we didn't wait at all when we got there. Before she got a word out, a nurse put out her cigarette and said, "Follow me and you can lay her in this room." Before the nurse had the bandages cut off and my face washed, a doctor was telling me he was going to take very good care of me.

"Have you ever had stitches before, Sydney?" His voice was quiet and gentle.

"No," was all I could muster.

"OK, well, there is only one part that is going to sting some. I'm going to give you a shot that will make it so you don't feel the stitches at all, but I have to be honest with you, the shot stings, OK."

"How bad does it sting?" I asked, but it was hard to move my mouth, so my words didn't sound very clear.

"I'm sorry to say, it stings pretty bad, but it's over pretty quick. I need you to do me a favor?"

"What is it?" I asked barely moving my jaw.

He laughed and smiled at my mom. "I like this kid. I don't know if I've ever had a kid ask me what it is first. They all just say OK." He turned back to me. "Even though it stings, I need you to hold still, and I mean perfectly still. Can you do that for me?"

I thought about it for a few seconds. He looked at my mom, and then back to me.

"Can I cry while I'm holding still?"

"Yes, it's a deal. You can cry, but hold still." He smiled, looking back and forth between my mom and me. "I'll be right back."

When he came back, he started washing his hands, putting on gloves, and getting lots of stuff ready on a tray. All the while, he was explaining what was going to happen. "First, I'll give you the shot. That way you won't feel any of the rest of what I have to do to get you all fixed up. Then, I'm going to wash out the cut so you don't get an infection. While I'm doing that, I'm going to look at your chin and make sure I don't see any other damage. But along those lines, I think an x-ray is a good idea given how difficult it is for her to move her jaw at this point. Don't worry, Sydney, those don't hurt at all, just a picture. But we'll stitch you up before the x-ray. From the looks of it, I'm thinking about ten stitches to get that chin all closed up. Should only take about twenty minutes. Do you have any questions?" He looked from me to my mom and back again.

I just shook my head. My mom said, "Will she need any antibiotics? Because she is allergic to penicillin."

"Nope, I don't see any real risk of infection, the washing is just standard protocol, so I'm not planning on giving her any antibiotics."

"OK, let's get started. Sydney, are you ready? This is the part we made our deal over. You get to cry if you want to, but you have to hold really still for me, sound good?"

I nodded. But it made me nervous when two nurses came really close and put their arms gently across my legs and shoulders as he started touching my chin. I couldn't see the shot, but the second he put it right inside the cut and squirted the medicine in, I let a scream out of me that would have made anyone think he was amputating at least two limbs. And of course, I moved my entire jaw in the process. Both nurses instantly tightened their grip on me and my mom held my head as still as she could; they were all holding me to the bed as he pulled the needle out for a fleeting split second of relief before he stabbed the needle back into the other side of the cut for another blast of torture, pulled it back out only to drive it directly into the middle of the wound again. He was quick, but I thought I might die it hurt so bad. I think it probably lasted about twenty seconds, but it seemed like at least three hours before he took the needle out of my chin for the last time and the nurses and my mom let go of me. He smoothed my sweaty hair back from my forehead and said, "I'm so sorry that hurt so bad, but I promise, that's the last thing you will feel.

85

Nothing else will hurt now. You did great." And he smiled. I just felt ashamed. I didn't keep my promise, and he was still being nice to me.

"Sorry," was all I could muster before I glanced away.

"Nothing to be sorry about. That hurts. I know! Now, we wait a few minutes for the numbing medicine to work, and I'll stitch you up good as new."

He was right. Nothing else hurt after that. The stitches were a breeze. The x-ray was nothing. I had a bandage that stretched from the side of one eye, under my chin, and back up my head to the side of the other eye. Plus, I was still covered in blood, which I was beginning to think was very, very cool. Turns out, I did crack my jaw too, but just a hair, so that would heal by itself. As we were leaving, I had the nerve to ask my mom if we could go to Dairy Queen for some ice cream, even though I was not really a great patient. The hospital is right across the street from a high school, where a football game had just ended, and the Dairy Queen was packed. I wanted everyone to see me, face bandaged, covered in blood. I knew they would all think it was as cool as I did.

"Sure, we can get some ice cream. It's probably the only thing you can eat for a while."

"But can we go inside the Dairy Queen and get it?" I asked, hoping she would say yes. The drive through would not really accomplish what I was after.

Glancing at her watch, my mom said, "Why not, we don't have to pick your brother and sister up for an hour. We may as well."

"Great! But can we stay there and eat it?"

"Fine, Sydney, we can stay there and eat it!" She knew what I was thinking and was getting irritated with all my questions.

Just as I'd hoped, when we opened the door to the Dairy Queen that had people in every booth and at every table and standing ten deep in each of the four lines, slowly everyone noticed the blood all over the front of me and the huge bandage on my face and started staring at me. We made our way to the back of one of the lines and started talking about what I could eat, when I noticed a man get up from a table he was sitting at with two kids and start rushing across the restaurant toward us. He looked very familiar, but I couldn't place him. He looked far more concerned than everyone else who had been staring at me. When he finally reached us, he grabbed my mom by the arm, startling her because she didn't see him coming like I did.

"Who's that?" I asked just as he got to us.

"What happened to her? Is she all right?" he asked at the same time I was asking who he was.

"Gus, what are you doing here?"

"Eating, but what happened to her?" he insisted. "Is she all right?"

"Yes, she's fine. She cut her chin ice skating and had some stitches. Come on, Sydney, we have to go. The line's too long." And she grabbed me by the arm, and marched me out the door. He just stood there staring after us.

"Mom, you said," I started to complain.

"Not now." She cut me off, and I understood by her tone she was not going to negotiate with me.

"Who was that man? Do we know him?" I asked glancing back at him standing there looking very worried as we walked away.

"Not now, Sydney," she snapped in a tone sharp enough to make me not ask anymore. I just climbed into the back seat and sulked. No ice cream, and I didn't get to ask any questions about the man who wanted to know how I was.

But I felt like we knew him.

I just couldn't quite figure out how.

When we walked back into the ice rink, the man who bandaged and carried me was the first person to see me. "Hey there, champ, how many stitches?"

"Ten," I said. But it was hard to move my mouth much between the bandage and the ache setting into my jaw.

"Wow, cool. That was quite a gash. Looks like you're gonna be back out on the ice in no time though, huh?" he said with a gentle pat on my shoulder.

I tried to smile, but my bandaged face wouldn't let me, so I just shrugged my shoulders. Ice skating was the last thing I wanted to do at that point.

Just then Mandy came up, "Syd, how are you, let me see! Did it hurt?"

"They gave me three shots right in my cut that hurt worse than anything in the world, but then I didn't feel anything after that. I got ten stitches," I said starting to revel a bit in the attention again.

"Mandy, can you please go find Mark and Bobby? It's time we get going."

"Sure, I'll be right back." Mandy wobbled over to the top of the stairs and yelled over the music, "Mark, Bobby, Syd and Mom are back! Time to go." Just like she did at home when it was time to call Mark for dinner.

My mom walked over to her, obviously irritated, and said, "Mandy, please don't yell. I could have done that. It would be better to go down to get them."

"Oh, sorry." And she shrugged her shoulders and went to

exchange her skates for her shoes.

Mark and Bobby came up the stairs and rushed over to me. "Hey, Syd, cool bandage. How many stitches did you get?"

"Ten," I said. "But the three shots hurt real bad."

Yeah man, tell me about it. I've had stitches five times, and those shots they give you are outrageous. But you'll have a gnarly scar," Bobby said.

"Come on, boys, go get your shoes. Let's get out of here before the session ends and they're swamped. 'Sides, I promised Syd some ice cream and if we hurry, we can get to Baskin Robbins before they close."

"Cool, thanks Mom," Mark said as they hustled off to trade their skates for their shoes. My mom ruffled my hair and winked at me. Normally I would have smiled back at her and tried my best to wink, and I couldn't decide if I didn't because of the bandages or if it was because I still couldn't figure out the man at Dairy Queen.

I sat up bolt straight in my seat. I was nine when I got those stitches. Gus hadn't seen me since I was five. That's four years and then the first time he sees me, I'm bandaged from ear to ear and covered in blood. No wonder he freaked out and we had to leave so abruptly. I wonder if he called my mom to find out what happened to me, and if I was really all right. I wonder if John knew. But I had no idea who he was. And he was sitting there with his other two kids.

Chapter Eight

As the dawn began to glow behind the eastern horizon, I fought to stay awake and ferret out any other times when I should have, or could have, known something wasn't right with the story that Ed was my dad.

"Hey, Mom," I shouted as I opened the front door after school that day in mid-December. "Moooom, where are you?"

"I'm right here," she answered, poking her head around the kitchen door that was visible at the top of the stairs right inside the front door to our split entry home. "You don't have to shout."

"I have some fantastic news for you tooo-day!" I announced, taking the stairs still carpeted in threadbare avocado green shag two at a time and tossing my coat and bag on the couch just inside the living room to the left, before joining her in the kitchen. "I'm so happy it's Monday and you're home, so I don't have to wait to tell you what happened today."

"What is it? How was your speech?"

"Weeeelllll," I said, dragging it out in dramatic fashion as I leaned my back up against the dark wood cabinet beside her and snuck a pinch of the lettuce she was chopping. "Oh hi, Mark," I said noticing him sitting at the table. "Why aren't you at practice?"

"I have a match tonight, so I'm home early."

"Oh, that's why Mom's already making dinner," I said

stealing some more of the lettuce she was chopping for what I assumed was to be tacos for dinner.

"Be careful there, missy. You'll lose a finger."

"I totally bombed my speech and lost the election. Kerry's the Secretary," I said.

"Oh, what happened? And how is that fantastic news?" she asked with a concerned look on her face.

"Well, you know how this dumb skirt and blouse used to be Natalie's?" I asked flipping up the side of the mint green pleated skirt I was wearing.

"Yeah," she said, still very concerned.

"Yeah, well she told everyone today that it used to be hers and that we're too poor to buy me my own clothes and so that's why her mom has to give me her old ones. So that made me really mad."

With that, she put down the knife and started wiping her hands. "I'm going to call Mary. That little brat. I cannot believe..."

"Wait a sec, Mom. Let me finish." She hung up the phone, but kept her hand on it, and looked at me. "Then, I was sitting there listening to Kerry give her speech. And she did a really great job. And I realized that I forgot to wear my bra today, and I got so embarrassed. I'm just not used to it yet, so I forgot. And I decided everyone knew and could tell, so I didn't want to go up to the mic and talk."

"Oh Sydney."

"Oh no, it gets worse. So when Mr. Angus introduced me, I walked up to the mic with my arms folded over my chest like this." I folded my arms across my chest to show her, "and just said, practically crying, 'Vote for me, I'll do my best', and ran off the stage. It was probably one of the stupidest things I've

91

ever done."

"Well, maybe not the stupidest, but it's up there," Mark said. I gave him a dirty look and stuck my tongue out.

She just stood there with a horrified look on her face for a few seconds, and then dropped her hand from the phone. "So, tell me how this is fantastic news?"

"Oh, yeah, that part. Well, Mrs. Stebril came and found me hiding backstage and let me stay in for first recess. Then, when Mr. Angus obviously announced that Kerry won, Mrs. Stebril picked me to be our class representative, so I get to go to the meetings anyway. Then, it gets better. At the first meeting today during second recess, she picked me to be Garbage Clean Up Coordinator for the whole school for the whole year!"

"What exactly does that mean?" she asked, still very concerned.

"Yeah, I know it doesn't sound that great, but it really is. See, I still get to go to the Student Council meetings for both the first and second half of the year. Kerry only gets to be Secretary for the first half of the year. And I make the schedule for each of the classes to take a turn cleaning up the playground each week. Then, I have to go to the teachers and let them know when it's their week, and like Mrs. Stebril said, it takes a really responsible person to be the Garbage Clean Up Coordinator. It is easy to be the Secretary. That person just writes stuff at the meeting they're already sitting at — no follow up at all. She said she believes in me and that I'm responsible."

She was finally smiling. "Well, congratulations then. I'm sure you'll do a great job."

"Um, that's not a thing, Garbage whatever," Mark said.

"Mrs. Stebril just made that up to make you feel better." I could hear the sarcasm mixed with pity in his voice before I looked and saw it on his face.

"Mark!" Mom said.

"I know that, Mark," I lied with lots of attitude dripping off my tone to make it convincing.

"Like I said, Syd," Mom chimed back in, "I'm sure you'll do a great job."

"Thanks! I'm sure I will too," I added taking another handful of lettuce.

"Now, let's think of ways to help you remember to wear your bra," she said with her chin down and eyebrows raised.

"Oh, why?" I complained. "I hate it. It's so uncomfortable, and the boys always run around at recess dragging their hand down your back to see which girls wear one and which girls don't. It's such a drag," I trailed off, making my way out of the room.

Then, Mark said, "I might get a shot at varsity Thursday."

"What?" my mom asked.

"Well, Pete's been really struggling to make weight lately, and coach said that if he doesn't make weight, it's mine. Which would be so cool 'cause Dad's gonna be here Thursday. He's never seen me wrestle before."

"Well, let's have Pete over for dinner!" I chimed in, which made everyone laugh. "Wait, this Thursday?"

"Yeah, why?" Mark answered.

"Well, 'cause this Thursday's my Christmas Concert, and I thought you and Dad were gonna come," I said looking to Mom.

"We are. The plan is we're going to go to Mark's wrestling match, which starts at five thirty, and then meet you at the

Christmas Concert. We can make both, don't you worry."

"But what if Pete is too fat and Mark wrestles varsity? Won't that be later?"

"Let's worry about that when the time comes," she said in a 'this discussion is over' voice. "Worrying about it now won't do anyone any good."

"OK," but I was worried.

When Thursday night rolled around, I was in my room putting on my red velvet Christmas dress my grandma made for me. My mom had already fixed my hair in a tight ponytail with a matching red velvet ribbon before she had to meet Dad for Mark's wrestling match. We still didn't know if he would wrestle JV or varsity. It all depended on if Pete made weight or not. But she promised me she and Dad would be at my Christmas Concert, and she promised me she would never break a promise to me. When I was ready, I looked at the clock. Six was still too early to leave for the short walk across the street to my school. We weren't supposed to be there until six thirty for the seven o'clock concert. So, I jumped up on my bed, scooted to the middle real careful so I didn't mess up my dress, and waited. The next time I looked at the clock, it only said 6.03. "Oh, for cryin' out loud, Mrs. B. I'm just gonna go." So, I hopped off my bed, put on my coat, and headed out.

"Whoa, where do you think you're going?" Mandy asked from the gold velvet chair where she was watching *Little House on the Prairie*. "You're not s'pose to be there for a while. It's too early."

"I know, but I can't stand it. Just let me go, please," I begged. "I can go visit my old teachers and stuff. You know, tell 'em about the garbage clean up schedule."

"Oh, fine," she said waving her hand.

On my way across the street, I decided I'd start with my third-grade teacher, Mr. Baker, then go see Mr. Jorgenson and Mrs. Storkson from fourth grade, then Mr. Sharp, and by then, it would be time to go to my class and Mrs. Stebril wouldn't be irritated that I was too early. I'd tell them all that my dad came all the way from Alaska just to see me sing tonight. And I'd tell them that I was the new Garbage Clean-Up Coordinator, just to make it seem more official that I was coming to their classes early. Each of my old teachers were happy to see me, and they thought my red Christmas dress and matching ribbon were very pretty. But they were really happy that my dad came all the way from Alaska to see me sing. They thought that was really something special. When I finally got to my class, most of the kids were already lined up, so it was easy to tell all of them that my dad was coming. They had never seen him before, so they were extra curious, which made it all-the-better. I told them he was really tall, so it would be easy to see him in the crowd, and he had really black hair.

Since we were the sixth graders, and the oldest, we filed in first so we could stand on the top row of the risers, which gave us a great view of the crowd. Twice, I bumped into the person in front of me because I was scanning the crowd rather than watching where I was going. But I couldn't find them. When I finally settled in my spot on the risers, I had a lot of time to search while the rest of the grades marched like drunk ants to their assigned places. My first strategy of randomly searching the crowd wasn't working, and I was starting to get a stomach ache. So, I took a deep breath, and reasoned with myself. You're just goin' too fast. Start in the back row 'cause they're probably a little late, and then work one by one until you get to the front. But by the time I got about half way to the

95

front, I was afraid they weren't coming.

"Well, where is he?" Pam whispered.

"I don't see them yet," I whispered back. "But they'll be here. My mom promised and she promised that she promised she wouldn't break her promise."

I didn't sing a word of one song. I just kept scanning the audience, row by row starting in the back and working to the front, and then from the front to the back. Then, I'd check each of the doors, and along the back row to see if they were standing. But each time, just like the last, they were not there. On my last scan, I caught Mrs. Stebril's eye and she saw that I wasn't singing and was looking all over the crowd. I expected her to give me a look for not singing, but she just smiled and nodded. I gave her a weak smile back. By the time we got to 'Silent Night' at the end of the concert, I had a boulder in my throat so big I couldn't swallow it down anymore. All I could think of, was all of the people I told that my dad was coming and how they would think I was lying, and that my mom broke her promise to me. I could taste the salty blood in my mouth from where I was biting my cheek to keep myself from crying. I felt so foolish for believing they would come, for believing what they said. When it was finally our turn to walk down the risers and file out of the gym, I ducked into the bathroom.

Each classroom was open for families to go back to after the concert and have punch and cookies. Locked safely in one of the stalls, I curled up on the toilet so no one would be able to see my feet under the door, leaned my head against the cold brick wall, and wondered how long it would be before everyone left so I could sneak home. It didn't take long for it to get quiet outside the bathroom because everyone bustled off to meet their children in their classrooms. With legs cramped from being drawn up to my chest for what must have been at least half an hour, I decided I could steal my way across the street in the dark. I would not go back for my coat hanging in my classroom alongside Pam's. But just outside the gym door, I had a thought that maybe they had come after the concert and were in my classroom waiting for me. But then again, I couldn't risk it if they weren't there. If I went to my class, and they weren't there, I'd be humiliated. If I went home and they did come after all, I'd miss my chance for everyone to see that I did really have a dad who came all the way from Alaska to see me. I decided to sneak around to the playground side of the building and try to peek inside the windows and see if they were there. I had to go around the back of the gym by the woods where it was as black as the coal my grandpa used for his stove, but that was the only way I could be sure no one would see me.

Rounding the corner of the gym, I whispered to myself that Jesus was always with me, no matter how dark it was and ducked low to creep under the bars, darted across the foursquare and basketball courts, and made it onto the slimy field. I was shivering, and my feet were getting wet from the grass, but it was worth not being seen. Standing on the sodden grass under the blanket of the inky December night, I felt the long dark hair on my arms standing up in the cold and the gravel sized bumps lacing my arms and legs. Before I started the last leg to the window, I looked up to the black sky in search of the moon or the big dipper. It was the only constellation I could identify, much to Mark's frustration after countless nights in the back yard where he patiently pointed out different constellations that I could never see, not even the little dipper. Dark clouds danced quickly across the moon like squirrels running across the road, but no stars were out. I let out a loud breath, noticing that I could see it for a fleeting second before the night swallowed it whole. More than my desire to see what I dreaded was a classroom full of other kids' parents, the cold setting into my body compelled me to start moving slowly and quietly toward the building. I was a long way down from the window itself when I felt the soft grass give way to the firm blacktop sidewalk. Good at sneaking quietly from all the times I snuck out of bed to watch TV from the hallway or crawl undetected in bed with my mom after I'd had a nightmare, I crept silently across the sidewalk to the edge of the building. With my back against the building, I slid along the frigid bricks, not caring about snagging my velvet dress, until I was at the edge of my classroom window. From there, I took another deep, disappearing breath and peered around the edge to see only a few people lingering around Mrs. Stebril's desk. My mom and Ed were not among them.

I pulled my head back so fast that it hit against the bricks hard enough to bounce twice, finally bringing the tears that had been threatening since we sang 'Silver Bells'. No longer being careful not to be heard, I ran back across the field and playground, around the back corner of the gym, through the cars snaking their way out of the parking lot, up and back down the other side of the hill in front of the school, to the corner across from our house. There, I paused behind the school sign, for if I crossed the street, surely someone in their car with their parents who did come would see me crossing the street alone. So, I crouched down, hugged my knees to my tummy to keep as warm as I could and pulled my arms inside my dress in the shadow behind the sign and waited until there were no cars left. When the road was finally quiet, I stretched my stiff legs and walked across the street, up my driveway, opened our front door, climbed the stairs, and turned to go down the hallway, straight to bed.

"Hey, where have you been? You should have been home a long time ago," Mandy yelled from the living room.

"I stayed and helped Mrs. Stebril clean up. I am the Garbage Clean Up Coordinator, you know."

"Oh, well I was about to come looking for you," Mandy trailed off as the commercial ended and whatever she was watching came back on.

I didn't answer. I closed my door to the precious hall light that I always wanted shining in my room at night, pulled the ribbon out of my ponytail and threw it on my dresser. It took some tugging and pulling, but I got my dress off by myself and threw it in the bottom of my closet, carelessly. Unconcerned about the little people I believed lived under my bed and came out at night to try and cut off my hands and feet, I stood with my feet half under my bed while I put on my nightgown, turned off my light, walked in the darkness over to my bed, and climbed in. It wasn't long before I heard my mom's car in the driveway, two doors slam, and the front door open and then close.

Her steps came up the stairs, paused for a moment when she asked Mandy, "Where's Syd?"

"I guess she went to bed."

"OK, well you need to turn that off and get to bed yourself. It's a school night, you know."

"Can I finish this show? Tomorrow's the last day before Christmas break and we won't be doing anything."

"Fine, but then straight to bed?"

"Yep. Hey, how did Mark do?"

"Well, he got to wrestle varsity, and he won his match. He was so happy, and it couldn't have been better that his dad was there to see it."

"Cool for him."

"Hey, how did Syd seem when she got home? I feel really bad we didn't make it to her concert. It would have been over by the time he was off the mat."

"I dunno. She just went right to bed."

And then her steps started coming down the hall. I closed my eyes when the hall light streamed in my room as she cracked my door. "Syd, are you awake? Syd?" She slowly came in and looked around. I heard her pick up my dress and hang it up and then go back out. She left the door cracked a sliver like I had been requesting every night of my life.

"Please close the door," I said in a voice barely above a whisper.

"Oh, so you are awake," she said, pushing the door open so the hall light washed over me curled in a ball, my back to my room. She came over and sat on the side of my bed. I didn't roll over to look at her, so she just rubbed my back the way I loved her to every night when I curled up on her lap to watch TV. "I'm really sorry we didn't make it to the concert. Mark ended up gettin'…"

"I know, I heard you talkin' to Mandy. Don't worry about it, it's not like I had a solo or anything." And I pulled away from her so she couldn't reach my back anymore.

"Well, I know you were excited for us to come, and so I am really sorry. It's just that this is probably the only time this year Mark will wrestle varsity, and his dad was here."

"Yeah, no problem. There'll be lots of other Christmas concerts this year. And I'm sure Dad will come again real soon. It's not like you promised or anything," I said sarcastically. After a few minutes, she leaned down and kissed my cheek.

"Syd, I said I'm sorry. I had a tough decision to make, and I couldn't be in two places at the same time."

"Yes, I know. I heard you."

"I love you, Syd."

"Night, Mom. Can you please shut my door?"

"I thought you were afraid of the dark?" she asked surprised.

"Not anymore. It's silly to be afraid of the dark. It's the same room in the dark as in the light, 'sides, at least Jesus is with me."

"I'll close it then," she said slowly with suspicion in her voice. "But if you change your mind, just call me."

"I'm sure I won't need you."

Several silent seconds hung between us before she pulled the door gently closed. I secretly hoped enough little people climbed on my feet when I was getting my jammies on and that it was dark enough under my covers for them to cut my feet off in the night so I could bleed to death. But then I caught myself thinking that and decided that was stupid too. I needed to stop thinking like a silly kid. No more hall light and no more stupid little people under my bed. 'Sides, Mandy gave me a great idea. Tomorrow was the last day of school before Christmas break. I was going to stay home from school. I already didn't feel very good. It was a perfect plan. And I rolled over and went to sleep.

That one also hurt, almost as much as the birthday disaster in Alaska. But by now, my cheeks were dry. Of course Ed stayed and watched Mark wrestle instead of coming to my Christmas concert. Why in the hell would he come to my Christmas concert? I wasn't his kid. I wonder if he would have even if Mark wrestled JV like he was supposed to. Doubt it, I thought. He'd have made up some excuse. I was so stupid.

Chapter Nine

My memories were coming fast now. I was so lost in them I hardly noticed when we stopped in the small towns along the way.

The bus that brought me home from middle school every day stopped right across from what was usually our empty driveway. My mom was always still at work, Mark was either at football, wrestling, or soccer practice — depending on the season, and Mandy was pleasantly asking folks if they'd like to supersize their orders at McDonalds most days. But on this particular day, both Mark and my mom's cars were in the driveway, which was concerning because the house had clearly not burned down. It had been a while since John left, but the familiar knot tightened in my stomach, and instinctively, I knew something was terribly wrong. I stood on the porch for a few seconds, afraid to open the door. Whatever was on the other side remained there as long as I didn't open the door. But knowing I couldn't stay on the porch forever, I decided to get it over with and slowly turned the knob. Mitsy, our little poodle, came to the top of the stairs, looked at me, and continued on down the hall way.

"That's not a good sign," I muttered to myself as I listened for any indication of what might have everyone home early. I also noticed a lot of smoke in the kitchen — I'm talking a thick fog that looked like the cold mornings on the Puget Sound when I used to go fishing with John, except this smoke was blue. The person my mom was on the phone with must have been talking up to that point because I hadn't heard any voices yet, but when I did finally hear her voice speak into the phone, I wanted to turn around and go back outside to the place in time before what I heard what she said, and the anger with which it was spoken, existed.

"If she doesn't want to live here with these house rules, she can find her own place to live. I'm done with this. Let her go to Alaska." I knew instantly, it was Mandy. I didn't know what or why, but she was in some kind of trouble. I knew she and my mom fought, kinda a lot, but it didn't seem serious. It was about doing her homework and chores and driving too fast and stuff. Nothing worth running away over.

I forced myself to take one step at a time and pass the turn to the hallway where my closet was waiting for me, but instead, I ventured the two more steps to the entrance to the kitchen and paused there. Mark was sitting at the table across from where my mom had obviously been sitting for a while by the ashtray full of cigarette butts, and the low burning cigarette she was nursing, but she was up to put the phone back in its cradle on the wall by the glass door. She noticed me standing there when she turned back to sit down.

"Oh, hi, Syd. Why don't you come in and sit down? We've got something up."

"Yeah, I heard a little coming up the stairs just now," I offered as I took a few steps inside the kitchen, but stopped to lean against the counter rather than join them at the table.

"Hey, Syd," Mark offered gently with a smile and a wink.

"Hey," I whispered back.

"Well, your sister's run away." And Mom started to cry. She sounded angry, but deeply wounded and shaken at the same time. "She left school today, drove herself to the police station, and asked them to place her in foster care because she doesn't want to live here anymore. I got a call at work from the Lynnwood Police, telling me that I would have to pay for her to be in foster care. I told them she can go live with her father if she doesn't like this home with its rules. So, she's down the street at the neighbor's until Ed can get here tomorrow and take her to Alaska." She spat out every word. I could tell she felt so betrayed. "What the hell has he done for her? Huh? That's what I wanna know." She sniffed long and loud, and wiped her eyes over and over.

"I'm sorry, Mom," was all I could muster, but I wanted to ask if I would get to see her, get to say goodbye, wondered if she wanted to see me, wanted to say goodbye. Or if she was just gonna leave. I really wanted to know why, but I didn't dare ask that.

"Oh, it's OK, Syd. Don't you worry about it. We'll be just fine," she sobbed out. But I did not believe her for a second. I smiled at her and nodded the best I could, fighting the baseball growing inside my throat, but I didn't think we would ever be fine again. After a while of silence, she left to use the bathroom, and I escaped to my room where I stayed until dinner. We got pizza, which was a rare treat that wasn't any fun. Mark's girlfriend, Christie, brought it over, and we ate in silence in the living room, which we never did.

We had just finished eating, Mark and Christie sitting on the couch that was along the wall opposite the top of the stairs. My mom was in one of the gold chairs just around the corner at the top of the stairs, and I was in the other gold chair over by the windows that overlooked the front yard, farthest from the stairs. Everyone was pretty quiet, and all you could hear was the tick, tick, tick of the wheel on the Wheel of Fortune spinning on the TV when the front door slammed against the wall as Mandy burst in, scaring everyone. It seemed like she was moving at the speed of sound because I saw her at the top of the stairs, at the same time I heard the door hit the wall. She grabbed my mom's chair, spun it around so they were facing each other, and accused, pointing in her face, "You're a fucking liar!"

Mark's response was instant and fluid. He sprang from the couch, arm swinging. He was mostly behind Mandy, so she didn't really see him coming until the last second. She turned her head just as his open hand struck the side of her face, and she disappeared from my view. It sounded like when I dumped a bucket of water out my second story window and it all hit the driveway at once. My mom just turned her chair back away from them both, curled her knees up to her chest and tucked her chin down. Mark stood over Mandy and growled, "Don't you ever talk to her like that again. She is our mother." I could not believe what I saw. Mark never hit anyone, for any reason, but especially me or Mandy. Boys were not allowed to hit girls. Plus, he wouldn't even get annoyed at us when we tried to irritate him. Like when we sat in front of him so he couldn't see the TV, just to bug him — he'd just quietly move over. And even though I'd heard that word, I'd never heard it in our house. Not even John said that, not even when he was drunk.

Mandy crawled away from him, used the end table beside the couch to help get to her knees, and then to her feet, and steadied herself with the wall leading to the kitchen. Mark's bright red hand print branded her left check. She looked from Mark to me to the back of mom's chair, stunned. "I'm leaving this place and living with my dad. Where's Syd gonna go when she finally realizes the truth about you people? Huh? Who's she gonna go live with?" And she stormed back down the stairs, slammed the door, and I didn't see her again for a long time.

Mark sat back down on the couch, rubbed Christie's knee to reassure her that it was going to be OK, and I slowly got up and went to my room to stand with my feet half way under my bed while I put on my nightgown and turned off the light for the night. Walking down the darkened hallway, I felt my anchors pull loose and start to drag across the bottom of my existence like when I used to go fishing with John and the current was too strong for our boat to hold position because he didn't have real anchors that were bought at the store — you know the kind that were steel with chains and with points that could dig in when the current was strong and the wind blew hard. He made his own by filling an old coffee can with cement and putting a rope inside when it was still wet so it would hold all right if it was a regular day, but not so good if it got rough at all. And he always had to make new ones 'cause the rope would rub on the side of the can, or just rot. Lying in bed, my stomach hurt real bad. It felt like something curdled inside me, like warm milk. It had been a while since I held Mrs. B. and talked to her — that was for babies — but as I got undressed and redressed, I instinctively said aloud, "Mandy's leaving, Mrs. B. Mark's going to college pretty soon. I don't know what I'll do without Mandy. And Mark." I paused for a long time and then added, "I feel pretty dumb, 'cause I thought only Dad's left, but I guess it can be anyone." After another long pause, I whispered, "I just sure hope Mom stays. That's all, I just sure hope Mom stays, Mrs. B., 'cause she could die like Aunt Marjie. Then I'd be real stuck."

As I tried to fall asleep, I did my best to picture the felt board from my first Sunday School class where the teacher showed how Jesus would leave all the sheep that were safe to go find the one who was lost.

I played this one over and over for I don't know how long. How is it that now Mandy asking where I'll go stands out like a chimney standing after a house burned down? At the time, I had no idea what she could mean? It didn't even occur to me that I didn't have the option to go to Alaska like she did, but somehow, I knew I didn't. Maybe I knew I'd never run away. Maybe I knew there was no place for me there and I had no place anywhere else. Maybe I knew I always had a place with my mom and I didn't need anything else. Mostly, I just felt so foolish.

Chapter Ten

My humiliation deepened as I remembered meeting Gus, like he was a stranger come into our lives. I was so embarrassed at the fool they all played me that I actually felt my face flush and had to bury it deep into my pillow, even alone at the back of the bus.

"Hey, Syd," my mom called from the kitchen. "Syd, come here a sec."

"Coming," I called back from my room, where I was changing clothes after softball practice. It was late February, and practices were so cold. "Hey, Mom, can I jump in the shower? I wanna warm up."

"Sure, but hurry. We're going out for dinner. You need to be ready in twenty minutes."

I thought to myself, since when are *we* going out to dinner. Why didn't we just pick something up on the way home from practice? Mark's not gonna be home for dinner, what's the rush? I wrapped my hair in a towel so it didn't get wet in the shower 'cause twenty minutes was not enough time to shower and dry my long hair. It'd have to live in the pony tail from practice. Whatever.

As I was grabbing my coat and heading out of my room, I heard a car pull into the driveway, so I propped myself on one knee on my pillows to peek out and see who was out there. For sure it wasn't Mark because his car sounded like a fighter jet and you could hear it at least a half mile away. There was a black Cadillac in the driveway. Wow, nice car, I thought to myself. The driver got out and headed to the front door. He was dressed in jeans, a sweater that I couldn't really see all of under his black leather jacket, and had on sunglasses even though it was pretty much dusk and a cloudy day. His dark hair was half gray, but he looked really pleasant, and very familiar. Quickly, I realized I needed to hustle out to the kitchen or he'd be inside before I had chance to ask my mom any questions. It was becoming obvious, this was who we were going to dinner with.

As I got to the end of the hallway, I realized I'd spied too long and wouldn't get a chance to interrogate my mom. She was opening the door.

"Hi, Gus, come on in. I think Syd should be ready. Let me call her."

"No need, I'm right here," I said as she was turning around to, no doubt, yell up the stairs for me.

"Hello, Sydney, I'm Gus. It's nice to meet you."

"Hello. Nice to meet you as well," I returned shyly.

"OK, well you've got your coat, so we're all set." My mom sounded very nervous. "I guess we can go."

Heading right back out the door he was still standing in, Gus said, "I was thinking we'd go to The Black Angus — you like steak?" looking at me.

"I don't know, I've never been there. But yes, I do like steak. Thank you.

Gently pinching my cheek, giving it a little giggle, and then dragging his hand under my chin and playfully slapping my other cheek — a gesture of affection I would come to know he does all the time to everyone — he asked, "How's your liver?"

"My liver?" I asked, looking at my mom for help.

"Don't worry about it," he said sounding like an Italian mobster from New York City, "It's just an expression."

"Oh," I mumbled, "it's fine, I guess," climbing into the back seat. His car was like my friend, Kari's mom's car. They were really rich, so I decided he must also be really rich to have the same car. They were also really nice, and so far, he seemed really nice. I thought only nice, rich people must have Cadillacs. We drove to the restaurant in relative silence. No one seemed to know what to say.

When we were seated, the waiter asked me, "Would you like something to drink?"

Answering like I always did when we were in a restaurant, "I'd like water, please," I was amazed when Gus chimed in with,

"Don't you want a soda or a Shirley Temple?"

"What's a Shirley Temple?" I asked.

Without even hesitating or looking to see how much they cost, Gus looked at the waiter, and said, "Please bring this lovely young lady a Shirley Temple with extra cherries. I'll have a diet cola, you?" he asked looking at my mom.

"Decaf coffee for me, please."

I started studying the menu for the cheapest thing, but everything was really expensive. This was not like Denny's where we usually went. I looked at my mom a few times for help, but she wasn't paying any attention. Gus noticed me glancing up at her and said, "Not sure what to get?"

"No, I haven't quite decided yet."

"You said you like steak, right?"

"Yes, my mom cooks us steak a lot."

"What kind?"

"Wow, I don't know." And I looked to her for help.

"Here, let me help you out. Have you ever had prime rib?"

"I don't know? Mom, do you make prime rib?"

"No, I don't. I make top sirloin."

"OK, well if you like steak, you must try prime rib. You'll love it. Just be careful of the horseradish they put on the side. That'll burn your nose hairs," he said with a playful smile.

I looked at my mom for help, but she was just looking at her menu, so I smiled and nodded. He ordered it for me, and it was absolutely the best food I had ever eaten in my life.

The night was spent with my mom and Gus talking about his business that I think has something to do with gambling, and Mark's wrestling, with a few questions directed to me about school and softball that I did my best to answer politely. As soon as we got back inside our front door, I peppered my mom with questions.

"Who is this Gus guy? Are you dating him and why does he know us so well?"

"He's an old friend from a long time ago."

"Well, are you dating him?"

"I don't know. Maybe."

"Maybe, what does that mean?"

"It means we're just getting re-acquainted and we'll see. Now, you better hurry up and get your homework done, it's a little late."

Not two days went by that Gus wasn't either at our house for a quick visit, or taking us out for dinner. He started stopping by my softball games and Mark's wrestling matches, which were getting more and more exciting. It was looking more and more like his dream of winning a state championship was possible.

Chapter Eleven
Homecoming Queen

"Aw, crap. Holly, I left my other bag in the locker room. You go on ahead. I'll see you tomorrow."

"You sure? I can wait."

"Naw, don't worry about it. It's already late, it'll only take me a minute to run back and get it."

"OK, see you tomorrow."

I turned and headed back down the stairs to walk to the gym that was at the back of our high school campus. The late September sun was just beginning to set, casting a pink shadow across the sky. There wasn't really anyone left around. The volleyball team was at an away game, the guys' team finished up a good half hour before we did, and the cross-country team was long gone. Football was still up on the field, but they'd be up there for at least another hour. The gym door echoed as it slammed behind me. Whenever I walked into the gym foyer by myself, I always glanced up at Mark's State Champion picture hanging in the hall of fame line up. I didn't expect to find anyone in the girls' locker room, so I was surprised to see Heather sitting on the bench when I walked in.

"Hey there. Whatcha doing here so late?"

"I should be asking you the same thing, damnit. I'm trying to sneak some homecoming surprises into you guys' lockers, but if you sneak back in, it's not gonna be a surprise, now is it?" Heather said with her voice full of attitude and her hands on her hips.

"Oh, sorry! I forgot my extra bag. I wasn't trying to *sneak* back in!" I said. "Your secret's safe with me."

"Thanks."

"Why are you doing this all by yourself? Shouldn't some of the other cheerleaders be helping you?"

"Yes, they should be. But the idiots only want to give stuff to the guys, so I'm here and all nine of the rest of them are in the guys' locker room."

"Football's still on the field; they're gonna get caught."

"They couldn't be happier if they did."

"Oh well, in that case, I'm sure they'll take their sweet time."

I grabbed my bag out of the locker and was about to leave when Heather asked me, "So, are you excited for the big assembly tomorrow?"

"Sure, I suppose so," I said.

"Uh, that was not so convincing." She mocked like a news reporter. "Sorry to interrupt Syd's busy life with a Homecoming Queen nomination."

Plopping down on the hard wooden bench with initials carved here and there that separated the rows of gun metal lockers lined up like rows of corn, I said, "It's not how it sounded. It's just that, I don't know. It's between me and Holly for one. And she's my best friend. So that's just tough. And really, I'd just be happier if it were her."

"OK, but you know how this works. One of you will be Queen and the other will be the Princess, so you both win either way."

"Yeah, I know."

"Geez, Syd. You don't sound like you want this at all.

113

There are dozens of girls who would love to be nominated. Ah, me for one."

"Wow, I'm so sorry. I know. I really am happy, or grateful. I don't mean to sound like I'm not."

"But you do. So, spill it."

"Well, I just have been happy with others winning it every year, that's all."

"Yeah, that's sucked every year. You've been the Class President every year since eighth grade, you have played varsity since ninth grade, you get amazing grades. I mean, come on, Syd. Every year people say, why didn't Syd get nominated for homecoming? 'Sides, Holly was Princess our sophomore year, remember?"

"Yes, I remember. And it was great."

"You're not telling me the whole story." Her gaze bore into me.

"If you win, there's half time at the football game. Every girl gets escorted out in front of the crowd and announced with her dad. I — do not have said dad."

"Oh, come on, Gus will escort you, right?"

"Of course he will. And he's great. But he's not my dad, and every single other girl will have her own dad. I used to go through this all the time in elementary school. There were constantly dad-daughter events and my mom would always find me a substitute dad. It was usually me tagging along with Natalie and her dad. It sucked."

"Let's be honest, that's because Natalie sucks."

"Well, that's true, but still. It sucks. I'd just rather be in the stands watching you and Holly with your dads out there."

"Well, too late for that nonsense. You're gonna win. And you deserve to win. So suck it up, put a smile on your face,

114

and let's talk about what's really important. What dress are you gonna wear?"

"Of course, that is what is really important. The dress! I'm gonna borrow Barbie's dress from prom last year. Remember the white strapless, silk dress with the big black sash across the waist that has a bow in the back?"

"Um, yes, Syd, I remember the dress. Everyone will remember the dress. You cannot borrow that dress. First, it's Barbie's dress. Everyone will know you borrowed it. Second, it's too soon. If it was from two or three years ago, maybe, but it's only September for God's sake. Prom was in May. What are you thinking?"

"I'm thinking I don't have a couple hundred bucks to buy a dress and I love that dress. I already borrowed it, and let's be honest, I don't have time to find another one at this point."

"All right then, Barbie's dress just became your dress. That's how we do this one."

"Glad to have you on board." We both laughed. "Well, I better get going. I have a ton of homework."

"Oh please, Syd. No one will care if you don't turn it in. You're gonna be Homecoming Queen tomorrow morning!"

"Thanks. But it has to get done sometime. Better now than later."

When I got home and opened the door, my mom was standing at the top of the stairs. Usually when I was late, she was worried, which instantly turned into anger for not calling to let her know I was going to be late as soon as she saw I was OK. But this time, she seemed really excited.

"Syd, where have you been? I've been waiting for you to get home. I have a surprise for you."

"Sorry, Mom, I left my bag in the locker room and had to

go back and get it. Heather was in there and we got to talking for a bit. What's up?"

"Come in here," she said, motioning for me to follow her into the kitchen.

I trudged up the stairs with my school backpack, soccer bag, and clothes bag in tow. "What's up? What's for dinner?" I asked almost simultaneously as I walked into the kitchen.

She was turning around with a long, navy velvet box in her hand.

"What's that?" I asked.

"Gus bought these for you to wear tomorrow and at the game," she said as she extended the box to me.

Dropping my bags at my feet, I slowly reached out my hand and took the soft box from her. I had no idea that jewelry came in velvet boxes, so I was baffled as to what might be inside. It was as soft as the underside of the dandelions I used to pick out of the neighbors' yards and try to sell back to them when I was young. At first, I pulled at the hinge side of the box before I realized I had to turn it around in order to open it. When I finally could pull apart the clam like container, I sucked in air like I'd been punched in the stomach. There before me was a strand of creamy white pearls with a delicate gold clasp on each end. The hand holding them started to shake a bit while the other instinctively covered my mouth. I wanted to look up at my mom for some kind of help in processing what I was looking at, but I could not take my eyes off them. Pearls were my favorite thing in the world — as far as jewelry goes. I had some really cheap, fakes in my room, but these were so much more delicate and the color was so rich.

Finally, my mom lifted the strand out of the tiny elastic belts holding it in place and clasped it around my neck.

"They're real pearls, so you need to be very careful with them, you hear."

"Are you kidding me, they're real?"

"Yep, they're real. He wanted you to have them to wear tomorrow."

"I cannot believe it," I said running my fingers over them as I hustled down the hall to the bathroom so I could see them in the mirror. I stared at them until my mom's voice dragged me back to the kitchen for dinner, but I wore them all night while I did my homework, caressing their soft round shape. Of course, I tucked them safely back in their navy velvet bed before I went to bed to not sleep that night.

The assembly to crown the Homecoming Court was a formal affair. Dressed in our floor length gowns, hair and make-up excruciatingly fixed, we waited in the locker room for the ceremony to begin. As it turned out, no one mentioned anything to me about borrowing Barbie's dress.

My mom and Gus were there. My boyfriend, Evan wasn't late, but shockingly early, and was perched right beside my mom in the front row. As we took our places on either side of the podium, I felt for the pearls that hung around my neck.

Waiting through the freshman, sophomore, and junior prince and princess announcements was excruciating. Sitting next to Holly made the tension all the worse. Ms Denson, the teacher doing the announcing, really botched the distinction between Princess and Queen with her announcement so badly that neither Holly nor I had any idea who had been named Queen until she came over and placed the larger crown on my head, long cape across my shoulders, and huge bouquet of yellow roses in my arms — all icing on my pearl covered cake. Parading around the gym with all twelve hundred students clapping and cheering felt surreal and almost distant. I was almost completely caught up in it all until I made it three quarters the way around the gym and got to where my mom, Gus, and Evan were clapping and cheering. My step caught, my smile froze, and I almost dropped the roses. My friend, who was King, noticed and helped me straighten the flowers, whispering, "You OK?"

"Yeah, just caught my toe," I lied. When I saw Gus, I remembered the game and facing the whole crowd with a substitute dad. I quickly regained my stride, focusing instead on what loomed ahead — a few days of being the center of attention in a magical way I couldn't even imagine.

When the second quarter of the homecoming football game began, it was time for me to change into my dress. With only the cement floored bathroom of the stadium available to change in, I had to be careful with the white silk gown I borrowed. My mom and my Aunt Linda, who fed my six-year-old self. Certs throughout my Aunt Marjie's funeral, were there to help me. I felt like I could have been a bride. Gathering up the skirt of my gown so it wouldn't touch the dirty floor, Linda cautioned me to step in slowly. Time slowed down as my mom zipped up the white satin and snapped the black silk bow across the back of my dress. With my straight brown hair brushed smooth and crown bobby pinned well enough to withstand a hurricane, my mom opened the navy velvet box and fastened my pearls around my neck. Draped with the black and gold silk cape, I took my place at the back of the line beside Gus and was ready to be presented to the audience as the Homecoming Queen. Being the last to be announced, I had a clear vision of each Princess and her father ahead of me. It was then I was thankful for the gusts of wind that cut through my silk adornments and could take the blame for the stinging tears in my eyes.

"Wow, that wind is really cold. It's making me feel like I have to go to the bathroom," I whispered to Gus.

"Go ahead, it'll warm up your legs," he whispered back.

I smiled at his joke, which alleviated the tension building in the back of my throat.

"Ladies and gentlemen, please stand for Lynnwood High School's 1985 Homecoming Queen, Miss. Sydney Rossler, escorted by Mr. Gus Papadakis." I strode out to the center of the platform, wind whipping my dress and crown, pearls adorning my neck, but the tears threatening to spill down my cheeks held in the back of my throat.

Chapter Twelve

The bus finally exited the freeway on Stewart Street in downtown Seattle. The Greyhound station was only a few blocks away, so I combed my fingers through my now greasy hair, straightened my shirt, and patted smooth my pillow. When it finally came to a complete stop at bay number three, I stood up and trudged my way along the narrow aisle lined with the velvet soldier-seats. As I stepped off the bus and started walking into the station, I heard a familiar voice call my name.

"Hey, Syd."

I looked up puzzled. No one knew I was going to be here. Standing off to the side of a bench, Evan gave me a small wave and smiled. I stopped in my tracks and stared at his warm smile and soft green eyes for a few seconds. I thought to myself, of course she called him. How was I going to face him? I smiled back and made my way slowly over to him.

"Hey there. What brings you down here?"

"Well, you know," he said, "I was just in the area and thought I'd swing into the bus station. See if I could pick up any girls."

I smiled and shrugged. Looking around I asked, "Having any luck?"

"Not so far, but my luck may have just changed."

"Oh, do you think so?"

"Yeah, I hope so. Can I buy you some breakfast? Maybe

you can tell me what has you getting out of the car on the freeway in Weed, California of all places and taking a bus back?"

"Oh, well, that's a very long story. And I'm exhausted. I don't even know where to start."

"Well," he said slinging my bag over his shoulder and gently tugging the pillow from my weary arms, "why don't we go get some breakfast, and you can start with what made you get out of the car on the freeway and go from there." He put his free arm around my shoulder and gently led me to his car.

The sun was just beginning to warm the day. We drove down Stewart to 2nd Avenue and then parked so we could walk down by Pike Place Market.

"Do you know where we're going?" I asked.

"Yep. There's a little diner down here inside the market. It has a nice view of the water. I made us a reservation."

"Wow. I don't think we've ever gone out to eat when you've made us a reservation."

"Well, I figured we might need a quiet table. I cannot for the life of me understand what has you upset enough to get out of the car on the freeway and take a bus home. Obviously, your mom called me, and she was very upset, but she wouldn't tell me anything. She said you are more upset than she's ever seen you and that I'll need to hear it from you. She's so worried." His voice was calm, but there was clear concern. "And I gotta be honest, Syd. I'm pretty worried too. That seems really out of character."

My head snapped fast and I said, "You have no idea what I'm dealing with here, so if you plan on lecturing me or judging me, save it. I can take a cab home to get my car."

The hostess looked up rather surprised and then

tentatively asked, "May I help you?"

Evan looked at her briefly and said, "We have a reservation. It's under Evan Hood."

He looked back at me with a puzzled look on his face while he waited for her to find it and gather up the menus.

"Right this way, please." And she led us to a small table tucked in a corner by a huge window with a mesmerizing view of the grey waters of the Puget Sound and snow-capped Olympic Mountains standing sentry behind. "I'll be back with some water, and your server will be right with you."

"Thank you," Evan said politely, but he never took his eyes off me. Uncomfortable under his gaze, I picked up my menu and started to look at the words without reading them at all.

"I'm starving. What is it, Saturday morning? I haven't really eaten anything since dinner Thursday night," I said.

"Syd, I'm not trying to judge you, and the last thing you'll get from me is a lecture. But really, what's going on? I'm more than a little worried about you."

"Let me find what I want to eat, and then I'll tell you."

We both scanned our menus for a few minutes until our server arrived with our waters. "Can I get you anything else to drink?"

"Yes, I'd like some tea, please. And I'm ready to order. Are you?" I asked.

"Yeah, I guess. You go first and then I'll be ready," Evan said.

"I'll have the buttermilk pancakes with fresh fruit, please."

"Would you like any sides with that? Bacon or sausage?"

"No thank you, just the pancakes and fruit."

"OK, and for you, sir?"

"I'll have the eggs benedict with fruit, please. No sides. Thanks."

"Would you like toast or a biscuit with that?"

"Oh, toast, I guess?"

"What kind of bread?"

I could see Evan was getting irritated with his questions. "Whatever you want."

"We have white, wheat, and sourdough."

Taking a deep breath, he said with a forced smile, "Let's go with wheat and no more choices."

Looking incredibly put out, he gathered up the menus and walked away with a curt, "Coming right up."

"Great, I'll have those right out."

As he walked away, I took a deep breath and tried to decide where to begin. Tears formed in my eyes. I took a deep breath and tried to steady my emotions with more deep breaths. Evan reached his hand across the table to take mine.

"Syd, what is it?"

"The short of it is my mom has been lying to me my entire life. Ed is not my father. She put the wrong name on my birth certificate."

"What the hell? Does she know who is?"

"Oh yeah, she knows. Gus is my father."

"What? Gus? As in Gus her boyfriend of three years, Gus?" He was clearly shocked.

I took a deep breath. It felt strange to say it. As much as I hadn't been doing anything but thinking about it non-stop since she told me, I hadn't actually said it out loud to anyone. The tears in my eyes started to spill down my cheeks. Before I could wipe them, Evan's warm hand was on my face, not wiping them, just cradling my cheek. I leaned into his hand for a few seconds while I gathered myself and looked up at him. I pulled my face away to blow my nose in my napkin.

Evan asked, "That doesn't make sense. Why wouldn't they tell you?"

"I don't know. She said something about they had an affair when she worked for him. She was separated from Ed, but Gus was married. She said I knew this until I was five and she thought I still knew it but just didn't want to talk about it. That's bullshit because…"

"Wait a second, how did you lose touch with Gus?"

"Oh that. She said when she left Gus when I was five, and she married John, some cops who Gus had turned in for taking drug money or something wanted to get back at him so they told him John was abusing me. So he tried to have John killed. That's when the police came and took us into protective custody. I remember that. We went to this crappy hotel and John forgot my bag with my Mrs. Beasley doll. I was so mad at him. Then Mark, Mandy, and I had to go to my aunt and uncle's house for a few days. I remember all of that. But I cannot remember ever knowing Gus, or knowing that he was my dad. And believe me, all I've done for the past seventeen hours sitting on that bus is wrack my brain trying to. I don't know what she expected me to do or say."

"Yeah, she seems pretty surprised at your reaction."

"What did she tell you?"

"Like I said, she called me and said she was trying to talk to you about something important and you got so upset that you got out of the car on the freeway and walked the rest of the way to the exit and got on a bus back to Seattle. I tried to get her to tell me more, but she just kept saying, please be there when she gets off the bus and try to talk some sense into her. She's just so upset, but when she calms down, I think she'll be all right."

Our food arrived and I was instantly so hungry. The bananas, peaches, and strawberries were piled high on top of three fluffy pancakes. I felt like I hadn't eaten in weeks. I smiled at the waiter and cut a bite. As soon as it hit my stomach, it tightened into a knot. I tried to take a sip of my tea to settle it down, but it just squeezed tighter. Evan was busily cutting his eggs benedict into bits and then stirred them all around in the golden hollandaise sauce.

With his mouth full, he looked up and said around the food, "You gotta admit, getting out on the freeway is a pretty bold move."

"I could not stay in that car with her one more second. She had this attitude like, 'you knew this and we were just honoring your wishes not to talk about it'. Like hell. She was covering her ass for having an affair and didn't want the mess following her around in the likes of me with Papadakis as a last name and a different dad. And I kept thinking back to all of the crap I went through thinking Ed was my dad. Do you know how mean he was to me? For starters, why would she send me to Alaska for an entire month to stay with him? I was only nine for God's sake?" I was starting to rant and caught myself. Looking out at the water, I tucked my chin in my hand to get a hold of myself. I could feel myself start to shake.

"Hey, it's going to be OK. I don't know how, but one way or another, we'll figure this out," Evan said. "I'm really sorry you're having to deal with this."

I looked back at him. He looked overwhelmed. "Thanks. I know I'll figure it out, but I just don't really know what's

125

next. It's a lot to work through."

"Yeah, that's for sure. Tell me more about these police officers. That sounds kinda like the mafia."

"I don't really know much more. They set him up to retaliate. I guess that's entrapment."

"And there was a trial and everything?"

"Yeah, I guess there was."

"How did you come to think Ed was your dad then? I mean, if you knew Gus was your dad until you were five, how did you make that switch?"

"I don't know. I can't remember that and I didn't really get that from her. She just said something like I wanted to be like my brother and sister and she let me. She thought it was best for me. I mean, I remembered going with Mark and Mandy to visit Ed. I somehow knew he wasn't my dad, but I don't remember knowing who was."

"So how did you leave it with your mom?"

"Well, like you said. I took a pretty bold step." And I smiled. "I insisted she stop the car. She didn't, so I opened the door on the freeway. That sorta freaked her out and made her pull over, and I got out and started walking. Thank God it was only about a mile to the next exit and there was a Greyhound bus station there. Otherwise, I don't know what I would have done." I half smiled and shrugged. "She followed along beside me the whole way shouting things out the window. It was pretty ridiculous, really." I smiled again, which gave him permission to laugh.

"Wow, I would have never thought you had it in you. You're such a people pleasing rule follower."

"Yeah, well, look where that has gotten me. Huh? My entire family has felt like they can just lie to me my entire life and keep massive secrets from me. Don't worry about Syd, she'll roll with anything."

"What do you mean, your entire family?"

"Uh, Mark and Mandy for sure knew this. They are old enough to know and now that I know what's up, I can think of times when they messed up, but I was just too stupid to figure it out. And all my cousins and aunts and uncles. My grandparents. I'm the youngest. Everyone knew. They all just played me the fool. Aw, don't worry about Syd, she'll just roll with it, she rolls with everything. No need to tell her the truth. What does it matter if she pretends Ed's her dad, like a little idiot? Do you know what it feels like it when someone lies to you? It feels like they think you're too stupid to know the truth. Like they either don't care enough about you to tell you the truth or don't respect you enough to tell you the truth. Either way, they sure as hell don't think you're smart enough to figure it out. And they were right. I didn't. So there you have it. I am the stupid idiot they all took me for. All this time I thought they loved me." I could see Evan was a bit taken back by the barbs in my words.

"Hey there, easy now. You weren't stupid. You were a little kid. There's no way a kid should be able to figure this out."

"Yeah well, I just feel incredibly stupid. I'm so humiliated. Like I'm just everyone's fool." Tears were running down my face again.

"Syd," he said gently. "Please don't be so hard on yourself. You are not stupid and you're not a fool. You cannot talk to yourself like that. It's just going to tear yourself down further." He paused for a moment. I just nodded my agreement. After a moment more, he added, "I thought you were hungry.

You've only taken one bite."

"I am hungry, but food is making my stomach hurt."

"Oh, well, I'm sorry. Are you sure you shouldn't try to eat something anyway?"

"I don't know. I honestly don't know what I should be doing."

"Well, I do. You should try to eat a little. You definitely need some food."

And so we ate in scared silence for a bit. Mostly, I pushed my food around to make it look like I'd eaten a little. But Evan ate.

"What are you going to do next," he asked.

"I need you to take me home to get my stuff and my car, if you don't mind. I can live at the sorority and finish my finals. I'll figure out what's next then."

"Sure, I can do that. You ready?"

"Yeah, I'm ready. I'm just going to use the bathroom."

When I came out of the bathroom, Evan had paid the bill and was waiting by the front of the restaurant for me.

"Do you want to go for a walk along the water?"

"Sorry, but no thanks. I'm exhausted. I'd just like to go home, sleep some, and get my stuff settled."

"OK, no problem. I can imagine you didn't get much sleep on the bus, huh?"

"Nope, not much sleep," I agreed.

Our ride to my mom's house was pretty quiet. I think Evan may have sensed what was coming. Maybe not.

As we pulled into my mom's driveway, Evan parked behind my little white Volkswagen Rabbit. "Can I help you?"

"No thanks. I'm gonna sleep for a bit before I do anything," I answered.

"OK, well when you wake up, call me. I can come back over and help you then."

"Evan, you must know, this changes everything for me."

"Well, yeah. I know."

"I mean, I am a mess. I gotta figure this out. And as you said yourself, I'm not really even acting rationally. Out of character, I think were your words."

"Syd, I think I know where you're going with this."

"Hear me out. It absolutely kills me to do this because you are amazing. I love you, so much. You were standing at the bus station waiting for me. I mean come on, that's pretty amazing. But this is no way to start a marriage. I'm a complete mess. My entire world just got turned upside down. I just got turned upside down. This wouldn't be fair to you, and it wouldn't be fair to our marriage."

Tears filled both our eyes. He looked at his hands sitting on his lap. I looked at the side of his downcast face.

He swallowed, and swallowed again. "Listen to me," he whispered in a hoarse, thick voice. "I'm with you in this. If you want to postpone the wedding, we for sure can. But hear me, I'm with you in this."

"I'm so sorry, there's just no way I can get married right now and I think I gotta figure this out on my own. I'm just so sorry," was all I could say as I pulled my pillow and bag out of the backseat and climbed out to trudge up the driveway. I couldn't look back. Instead, I distracted myself with the thought that it had only been like thirty-six hours that I came bursting through this front door ecstatic to get this road trip started.

I climbed the stairs, dragged myself down the hallway, and fell into my bed. It was a long time before I heard Evan's

129

car start and back out of the driveway.

After a fitful sleep, I woke up in the middle of the night. I knew I wouldn't be able to sleep anymore, so I packed all the rest of the clothes I'd left at home when I moved to school into the back of my car. I left a note for my mom on the kitchen counter.

The wedding is off. I trust you'll take care of the details.

Sydney

Chapter Thirteen

Normally my sorority would have been deserted so early on a Sunday morning, especially on a holiday weekend morning after the night's drunken blur of a good time, but it was getting close to finals week and holiday weekend or not, there was no more putting off studying or writing that paper. Girls were quietly getting breakfast, the only meal you were allowed to actually have anything to do with, being there was a lock on the kitchen door after the cook arrived at nine a.m.

"To what do we owe the pleasure of the company of our way too young princess bride so early?" Gina's sarcastic voice grated at my raw nerves, but I ignored her. I'd barely spoken to the girl until my engagement was announced and ever since she sought me out like a lioness after a wounded antelope. I don't know if it was pure jealousy, or if I'd actually done something to incite her wrath, but I wasn't in the mood for it that morning having just left my mom the note telling her to cancel the wedding, and I wasn't up for all the questions announcing the wedding was cancelled would bring.

"So, let's see the rock. I bet you've been up all night polishing it so it shines just so." Usually by now someone shut her down, but everyone was too distracted with themselves to interject. Her scan of the room found no one even paying her a crumb of attention. Unwavered by the lack of an audience, Gina kept pushing. "Now that I think about it, we never see you here on a weekend day. Always home with dear Evan for church, or are you too ashamed to go? Maybe that's it; you've been practising the wedding night thing and can't show yourself in church?" She looked at me with a condescending smirk. With that, I heard someone take in a heavy breath indicating she may have gone too far. The room fell silent. The only sound to be heard was her knife scraping half melting butter across her golden toast. "That's what I thought," she continued when I grabbed her arm and spun her around to meet my steel gaze an inch from her face.

My eyes were eerily vacant as I said in a low, steady voice, "You will never speak to me, or about me again. You understand?" As I waited my grip tightened around the soft, pink flesh of her upper arm. My nails dug deeper until I felt each one puncture the skin on the inside of her upper arm and I could feel a small trickle of blood seeping between my fingers. She whimpered in pain. "That was not rhetorical. I am waiting for an answer. I mean to say, if you are in a room and I enter, or even if someone else is talking about me, I don't care what you're doing — if you've just poured milk on your cereal — you get up and leave it, if you are sitting in a stall halfway through taking a shit, you will get up and leave without wiping. Do you understand me? You will never speak to or about me again." She just stared at me in fear. I dug my nails deeper and more blood dripped down her arm. My eyes and voice held steady and low. I don't know if she felt more horror or fear, or if it was just the pain of my fingernails tearing into her arm, but finally she nodded an agreement, and I released her arm, turned and started toward the backdoor without saying another word to anyone. I could hear the silence of the room behind me in the rush of my thrashing heartbeat pulsating in my ears. The clap of the screen door broke the spell and everyone burst into commotion behind me as I trotted down the steps.

I heard her start to say, "Did you..." when another voice said, "Oh give it a rest, Gina, it's about time someone shut you up."

I needed to hear the methodical lapping of the lake, and sit in the peace of the morning sun, warm and comforting like a loaf of bread a moment out of the oven. I felt as if my entire life had been smeared with olive oil and I was trying to bare-handedly keep it from slipping over the edge of a cliff. Sitting on the grass, still wet enough with dew to make my butt damp after a bit, my head hung between my knees. Finally, the shock and rage inside me gave way. It started like the tiny hole in the dike the little Dutch boy lied about, but slowly the tears streaming silently down my cheeks gave way to sobs. I let the waves of emotion wash over me. I was deciding to finish my finals, pack up my car and disappear. Tell no one where I was. That would make them all crazy with worry, forever. After completely exhausting myself, I tipped my head toward heaven. I didn't even want to ask why. What did it matter why? Asking why seemed arrogant, as if I alone deserved to be answered to for my pain and mistreatment. I wondered what God did with all those 'why' questions? If they were raindrops, they would overflow the ocean. Do they annoy him? They were annoying me. Rather, I just gazed out at the lake and Mount Rainier standing sentry, and the sheer strength and beauty of it gave me such comfort, and wondered how I could ever get myself back. I need to know the way back to who I am. You know, to Sydney who is sane and doesn't hurt people and get out of moving cars on the freeway, and I don't know. I just need to find my way back. Then, quietly, I knew God spoke to my heart. It wasn't something mystical, but instead soft and tender, almost so soft the sound of the still morning water could have drowned it out.

"There is no peace in vengeance, only in forgiveness. If you do this, you'll hurt them, sure, but really, it's your own life you'll ruin, and break Evan's heart. The way back is through forgiveness."

For the first time since Friday afternoon, I felt an easing rather than a building inside of me. It felt like a warm beam of sun caressing my cheek and relaxing my tense shoulders that had been cold too long. I lay back, closed my eyes and fell into a childlike sleep. The weariness of anger had caught up to me, and I couldn't sustain it any longer. I don't know how long I'd been there when Evan's gentle touch and soft voice brought me back from my slumber retreat.

"Hey, I've been looking all over for you."

Opening my eyes to his forehead pinched by worry, I whispered a sleepy, "Hi. How did you find me?"

"It wasn't easy, believe me. I went to your house this morning and your mom showed me the note you left. She's pretty distraught over all this."

"Wow, she's home already?"

"Yeah, apparently she left right after Mark's last match and drove straight through the night."

"Thank God I got out of there early. She's the last person I need to run into right now. Did she say how Mark did?"

"Yeah, he won. He'll be on the World Team."

I smiled. "Oh, that's great. I'm happy for him."

"Yeah, that's great. Listen, Syd. Your mom's a mess."

"Yeah, I can relate," I said sitting up. I wasn't about to let him start feeling sorry for her.

"I bet. So, then I went to your sorority and Kris told me about the kitchen incident and that you left. Next, I went to all the libraries we usually study in, but of course, you weren't there. This was my last idea before I just camped out at your sorority and waited for you to come back."

"I'm glad you came."

"I wouldn't want to be anywhere else."

"You sure? It's pretty ugly around here." I held up my hand with Gina's blood still under my fingernails. He pushed my hand down.

"Are you kidding, the view is incredible."

"I wasn't talking about the lake."

"I know, I know. You look like you've been through a war, but you know how I get lost in those brown eyes."

We sat in the still drying grass, Evan's arm around me holding me to him. We were both a bit afraid of where to venture next. Conversation seemed like a minefield. Finally, I broke the silence.

"Do you know what God's voice sounds like?"

"Yeah, I think I've heard it once for sure."

"Really, what did it sound like?"

"Well, it's a pretty good story actually. I've never told you before because I didn't want to scare you off."

"Oh, do you think I scare easily?" I asked the question without realizing the double meaning.

"No, not really. You might be one of the toughest people I've ever met. You see, just over two years ago I was riding my bike, through here actually, and I prayed what seemed like a ridiculous prayer. It was for an outgoing, athletic, smart, not fat, girlfriend who had a fantastic smile. I emphasized the smile part. I really wanted a big, toothy smile. One that really grabs your attention, you know. Crazy specific prayer. About five hours later, I was at Lynnwood High School giving a presentation for the Business School, and you walked in, late, and I'm sure God said, *there's your wife*. And then, you smiled at me. One of your biggest smiles, I might add. It was huge, all teeth and gums. I started stammering and completely lost my place in my presentation. I thought, slash, prayed, *whoa there, I prayed for a girlfriend*. God said again, *there's your wife*. Totally freaked me out. And it took me a long time to find my place in my presentation again."

"I remember that. I felt bad 'cause we walked in late and I thought we messed you up by interrupting you."

"Trust me, you did mess me up. Never quite been the same since. You see, I had become a Christian about nine months before and then dated a slew of really weird Christian girls — I'm talking fat, I wanna be a missionary in Africa- weird. It was really freaking me out because I thought I was going to have to marry one of them."

I looked at him warily. "A slew of girls?"

"Yep, you know me, a real ladies' man." With his head cocked to the side so I could see his crooked smile. "No, I promise, that's the truth. The prayer part."

"You can't pray like that. God doesn't take orders."

"No, not really. I know that now, but that's the way that went down."

I looked at him and there were tears forming in the corners of his eyes, which brought more to mine.

"So, you see," he went on slowly, "I understand you're struggling right now. God knows I would be. What your mom dropped on you is huge, and would really throw anyone. Obviously, I can't make you marry me, and I don't want to — make you that is, but I'll wait. I think we can get married in three weeks and get through this together, but if you want to put it off, I understand. But please, don't push me out. I want to help. I love you and I can't bear to see you endure this alone."

It took a while for me to find my voice, but as promised, Evan waited. "Well, sitting here this morning I looked to heaven and wondered how I stop this spiraling. I've been through a lot in my life with John and Ed and all their abuse, but I've never felt this out of control. I looked out at the lake and the mountain, and I thought to myself, how do I get back from here? I didn't even ask and I think God spoke to me. I don't know how, but somehow, I'm going to have to find a way to forgive — all this. All of them. I keep thinking of more people. My cousins? Did they know? My grandparents. For sure they knew. But finding more people to be mad at isn't helping. I was so comforted by the lake and the rhythm of the lapping sounds and the mountain standing there reflecting the sunlight. I was tempted to ask why me, but that felt so annoying. On the bus ride I saw the sunset and then rise and then this morning, I was up early again and saw the sun rise. You know what, it'll set again tonight. The thing is, this lake and that mountain will still be here no matter what. The sun will rise and set every day, no matter how mad I am or what I do with this. It's all so much bigger than I am. Who do I think I am to demand an account from God? You know? It seems pretty arrogant. I can throw a fit and scream and yell. Or, I can know they screwed up because they were probably in a place just like I am right now because someone, maybe their parents screwed them over, and they chose to be mad about it and then stormed off to do a bunch of justified shit that only made things worse and hurt more people. It won't be easy; I don't even know the whole story. You know, 'cause I just up and got out

137

of the car on the freeway." We both laughed a bit. "But one thing I've figured out is that I don't want to make you a victim in all this and lose the one person I can trust." A long, quiet moment hung between us before Evan finally spoke.

"So, June 27th it is?" There was playful hope in his voice.

"Yeah, but you should know, I have issues."

"Yeah, I know. Believe me, I know," he teased.

"I need you to talk to my mom about this. I can't face her right now. And maybe after finals, can I move into our apartment and you stay at your mom's, until the wedding? I am not moving back home. That would be way too much, way too soon!"

"I can do that as long as it isn't just one more thing. I'm in this for the long haul with you."

"Thank you."

We lay back on the grass and I let the peace of God's voice, the warmth of the morning sun, and Evan's embrace comfort me.

After a long time of silence, I said to him, "I feel like I've been sitting in a bathtub filled with really gross water, you know soapy, dirty, nasty water. Like after you shave your legs."

"Nope, don't know 'bout that."

"Well, trust me, it's not great. And I've been sitting in it for three days, just pruning up my whole body. Sort of marinating in rage. But this morning, sitting here, I feel like I pulled the plug and the water's starting to drain out."

"That's awesome," Evan said enthusiastically.

"Well, don't get too excited. It's gonna be slow. You probably also don't know about tubs with plugged drains with your short hair and your rich house where everyone has their own shower. But in my house, all of us shared one tub, and us girls have a lot of thick hair. The drain gets clogged, a lot. John used to get so mad. He'd yell at us all the time, 'get the screwdriver, pop that plate, and pull your nasty hairball out of the damn tub'. Let me tell you, a hairball in the tub drain, is the worst. Even when it's your own hair. It's just under the drain plate, and you have to reach in there and get a hold of the top of it, but when you start pulling, it's huge. Like six inches of nasty, shampoo and conditioner-matted mess. And oh God, the smell. It's like pond scum with some garbage and clam juice mixed in. It makes you gag. And the thing about it is, as soon as you pull it out and put the plate back on, it just starts building again as soon as someone takes another shower. When it's clear, the tub drains really fast and stays pretty clean. It's nice. But when it's clogged, it drains really slow, and the sides of the tub are a soapy, nasty mess."

"What are you getting at here, Syd?"

"I'm just sayin', I think this, this, I don't know what you call it, mess, thing, with my family. It's a hair clog that is gonna keep coming back. There might be some clean tub times when the water drains fast. But I have a feeling, I'm gonna have to reach in and pull out the nasty, sticky clump a lot."

"Yeah, well, I'm pretty handy with a screwdriver."

"That's sweet, but this is my clog, and I have a lot of practice with hair clogs. I do, sometimes, need help recognizing that it's time to pop the drain and pull it out though. It's easy to get used to standing in my own dirty water."

"I'm happy to let you know, and help with the clogs. No matter how messy they get."

"I thought you'd say that." And I rolled on my side and tucked myself into Evan's side even deeper.

Chapter Fourteen

I don't know what Evan said to my mom, but she gave me the space I needed. It was in Tuesday's mail that the only communication we had about the topic for months came. Her note read, 'I can only hope you know I love you and always have. I did what I did because I believed it was the best for you. If you have any questions, please come to me, and I will answer them. Love, Mom'.

I made a list of all the last meetings we had planned with the florist, rental company, reception hall, piano player, wedding coordinator, and her friends who were making all the food for the reception. I would go to all the meetings on my own, except for the one with her friends. She could do that. If I was going to concentrate on my finals and not tank this quarter of school, and then have any chance of holding it together for the wedding, let alone enjoy it, I needed to put this whole thing aside until after.

I didn't see Gus until just before the wedding. I didn't know what to do or say. We were hosting a dinner at Lena's for Evan's dad, in town from San Francisco for the wedding. It was Gus's favorite Greek restaurant. We'd planned this long ago, thankfully, or I don't know how we'd have managed the communication necessary to put it together. Evan picked his dad up at his hotel and then came to get me at our apartment. He left his dad waiting in his tiny copper colored Honda Civic and jogged up the four flights of stairs to get me. On the way to the car, I asked him what I should say to his dad to try and make him like me.

"Oh, just be yourself. He'll love you."

"That's not helpful, Evan. He already doesn't like me. He already wrote you that letter telling you he thinks it's a bad idea for us to get married, so there's that," I said with a nervous sort of laugh.

"That's just him trying to pretend like he's being a dad. He hasn't done anything dad-like in my life since, well, practically, ever. Don't you dare let him intimidate you with his stupid letter."

By then, we were outside and I could see Evan's car, but nobody was inside it.

"Where is your dad?"

"God knows?" And we started looking all around. "Oh, there he is." Evan pointed across the parking lot to the side of the building. A very tall man with mostly gray hair was walking out from between the buildings with his hands clasped behind his back looking as if he were inspecting the place. Evan opened his car door and lifted his seat so I could get in the back.

"Aren't we going to wait for him?" I asked, confused.

"Yeah," Evan said, clearly irritated. "We'll drive over there and pick him up. He cannot sit still for five minutes, so I'm sure he decided this would be a good time to take a walk."

"Hmm," I said, "Sounds like someone else I know."

"Very funny," Evan grumbled as he pushed his seat back into its place so he could get in and drive over to where his dad was. It was clear he saw us get into the car, but he just kept wandering on his course and didn't bother to head our direction. When we pulled up alongside the walkway where he was, Evan stopped and he nodded casually as he made his way over to us. When he was fully settled in his seat, he turned around to look in my direction. I put my hand out to shake his and started to say, "Hello, Mr. Hood, I'm Sydney, it's ni…" when he cut me off.

"Yes, clearly, I know your name, young lady. You're welcome to call me Fred. It will be uncomfortable for me to contort my body to adequately shake your hand so please wait until I'm in a proper position to execute that greeting."

"Oh, I'm sorry, yes. I didn't think of that," I stammered as I withdrew my hand. I felt my face reddening.

"No need to apologize. It was a nice gesture that I will return when I am able. Now, where is it that your family would like to take me to dine?"

"Well, it's nothing fancy, but my mom's boyfriend, or my, uh," I looked at Evan for help as I was really having trouble with my words. I hadn't had to label Gus for anyone yet.

"Syd's mom is dating Gus, and he's Greek. He knows of a really quaint little Greek restaurant with authentic Greek food. I told them how much you like authentic, well-prepared food, so we picked this place."

"That sounds lovely. And this Gus, was he born in Greece?"

Evan looked back at me to see if I was going to answer. I spoke up, "No, he was born in Seattle. His father came here first, just after the First World War. Then, when he'd established himself well enough, he went back to Greece and married a girl from the tiny island he was from. They had a daughter there before the three of them came back. Gus's older brother and he were born here."

"And what was their life as Greek immigrants like?"

"You know, I've heard plenty of stories, but you should really ask Gus. He loves to tell those stories and he'd do a much better job than I."

"You speak very well."

"Oh, well, thank you."

"Do you know why I complimented your speech just there?"

"Oh, come on, Dad, don't start grilling her on grammar."

"She is an English major, is she not? She and I can have an intelligent conversation regarding the spoken language."

Evan gave me an apologetic look in the mirror.

"I think you noticed that I said 'he'd do a much better job than I'. Most people would say better than me."

"You are absolutely correct. Most people would say that. And you did not. Do you know why you did not?"

"Yes, in fact I do. That's why I did not say, me," I answered. I knew it was a bit of a sassy answer, but nervous or not, anxious to win his approval or not, I was not about to put on a dog and pony show for him. He was starting to irritate me.

Fred looked at Evan with a wry smile, "A bit of a backbone to that one, huh?"

"Yep, that's just one of the things I love about her."

"Say, do you read any William Buckley?"

"Oh, Dad, please. Do not start asking her about Buckley."

"I'm sorry, I do not. Do you by chance read any Virginia Wolf?"

"Oh yes, we'll get along just fine, she and I," he said. Evan raised his eyebrows at me in the rearview mirror. I raised mine back at him and looked out the window.

Fred asked Evan all about his job selling computers for

the rest of the ride while I tried to imagine how someone as outspoken and strong willed as Evan's mom could have ever been married to him.

When we arrived at the restaurant, my mom and Gus were waiting for us inside the door. It was the first time I saw him, knowing, I guess it's knowing again, that he was my dad. I didn't know how I'd feel. When we walked inside, my mom went straight to Fred and introduced herself. I didn't hear much of that. Evan was involved in that conversation, helping with the introductions. Gus and I were behind them. He put his hand on my cheek, gave it the same familiar pat and pinch he always did. He looked at me and let his hand linger on the side of my face, which brought warm tears to my eyes, before Evan said, "Dad, this is Gus, Gus, this is my dad, Fred."

Gus dropped his hand from my cheek to extend it to Fred and turned his attention to the introduction. Gus was his usual warm and jovial self. As awkward as I felt, on some level I enjoyed thinking of him as my dad. I had spent at least an hour every day since that Sunday on the shore of Lake Washington praying through forgiving each and every member of my family. And each day felt like I was starting over. But then, when I saw him, I could tell it had helped. The rage had subsided. In some ways it didn't seem fair. He was the one who was absent my whole life and I probably should have been angrier with him than I was with my mom. But then she was there every day to inflict the harm and well, he wasn't.

Evan's dad grew up on the streets of New York, a small child in an Irish immigrant family. After his father abandoned his brother and him, Fred began working at anything he could to help feed the family. He and Gus traded stories of making their way in America, engrossed by each other's struggle. The fascination and familiarity of experience took over protocol for a first meeting, and their conversation carried the evening, much to my relief. By the time Evan dropped me back at our apartment and left to take his dad back to the hotel, it was well into the morning of rehearsal day, and I fell, exhausted, into bed.

Not only was staying at our apartment giving me peace of mind, but I'm not sure where I would have stayed had I been at my mom's house. Mark and Christy were in my room, my sister and her husband Mark, in hers, and my aunt and uncle downstairs in my brother's room with my cousin on the couch. That would have left me to sleep with my mom. It had always been a place of comfort I ran to when I had a bad dream in the middle of the night. I slept with her for months after coming home to find two men robbing our home just a few years earlier.

The phone's third ring dragged me out of sleep early Friday morning. Groping for the phone, my voice betrayed my sleep.

"Hello," I mumbled rubbing my face hard.

"May I speak to Sydney?" the reservation in my wedding coordinator's usually cheerful voice snapped me awake.

"This is Sydney. Is this Donna?"

"Yes, Sydney, I'm afraid I have a bit of bad news. The church decided they don't want you to move the piano off the stage for the wedding tomorrow because there won't be time to have it tuned again, for services or the conference they're holding next week. I'm sorry for the last-minute notice, but I think we can make it work."

"No, we can't leave it up there. We are going to have three hundred candles up there, plus flowers and twelve bridesmaids and twelve groomsmen. There's no way we'll all fit. They can't do this on such short notice. I'd have ordered fewer candles and flowers, but they said no problem."

"I know and I'm sorry. I hate to be the bearer of bad news. I have some ideas of how we can make it work. Can you get to rehearsal a bit early tonight so we can work them out?"

"Yeah, I'll be there about six, is that early enough?"

"I was hoping for four or four thirty really. This isn't going to be easy. In order to fit the five hundred guests you're expecting and all the wedding party, we're going to have to be creative."

"Our rehearsal dinner starts at four thirty. I need to be there for a little while."

"Oh, that's right, we'll just have to make it work at six then. I'll be waiting for you."

"OK, bye."

Flopping my head back on the pillow was my first realization that it was so late. Glancing at the clock, I expected it to be early by the way I felt, but it was well past ten. I had no idea how little sleep I had gotten and it was finally catching up to me. I have a sneaking suspicion that all brides are a bit emotional just before their wedding, but this news brought more of the tears I felt like were bottled up inside me just waiting for a reason to break like the spillway of a dam opening.

I pulled myself out of bed. Sitting on the toilet with one knee touching the cabinet and the other the bathtub in the tiny bathroom, I remembered we were going to decorate the reception hall at nine that morning.

"Damnit." I hit my knee and reached over to turn on the shower. If I was fast, I could make it there with plenty of work to be done. I'd just throw my hair up real quick and then shower again and get ready before rehearsal later. Within fifteen minutes, I was in my car on my way to the reception hall. If I hurried, I'd be there by eleven. Surely, they wouldn't have everything done by then.

But as I was pulling in the parking lot, I passed my mom, Christie, my aunt, my cousin, and my brother-in-law pulling out in my mom's car. She waved and kept going, which struck me as odd. She would normally have stopped. Mark and Mandy were standing on the steps chatting. I pulled up beside the stairs and rolled down my window.

"Hey guys, sorry I totally overslept. Is everything done?"

"Nothin' to be sorry about. You deserve some sleep. We got it," Mark said.

"You wanna come in and see if you like everything?" Mandy asked as she started walking back up the stairs.

"Sure," I said, clearly disappointed. May as well. And I turned my car off, got out, and followed them into the community center. "Where was everyone else off to in such a hurry?" I asked.

"Oh, nowhere, just heading back home," Mark said looking at Mandy.

Standing in the doorway, I could not believe my eyes. The building is divided into two separate rooms with a large foyer in the middle. That's where we were standing. In front of us were two large tables. The one to the right had a huge chocolate fountain and lots of empty silver trays where there would be fresh fruit and marshmallows. Of course it was covered with a peach table cloth with a white lace table cloth over the top of it. There were little peach plates with a fanned-out stack of napkins with Evan and Sydney, June 27, 1987 printed in gold cursive writing across them. The table to the left had a tower of champagne glasses and a champagne fountain waiting to be filled and turned on. There were more printed peach napkins fanned out.

From the center of the ceiling hung peach and white netting that stretched out to each corner. I looked to the large room to my right and there were dozens and dozens of round tables all with white table cloths. They each had three small candles circling a vase with peach roses and greenery. The long table under the windows at the front of the room was set up for the food. There were stacks and stacks of plates and more printed napkins. This room also had the peach and white netting hanging from the center going out to each of the four corners. The large room to the left had a few more tables, but there was a large empty space for the band and dance floor.

"Hey, close your eyes," Mark said. "OK, are they closed?"

"Yes, they're closed, but what are you doing?"

"OK, now you can open them."

I sucked in a huge breath of amazed air. "Wow, thanks you guys. It looks fantastic." We hadn't planned to, but they found a way to put tiny white lights inside the peach and white netting in the ceiling and it looked just magical.

"Oh, I'm so glad you like it. I think it will be so much better when it's dark, but the lights really make it pop, don't they?"

"For sure. They are amazing. I really can't thank you guys enough. I feel really bad I wasn't here."

"Sure thing. It was fun. We only had one tiny glitch. The cake top thing has a cross hanging from the heart that goes around the bride and groom. The little glass cross fell off and we can't find it anywhere," Mandy said apologetically.

"If that's all that goes wrong, we're golden," I said. "No one will miss it."

"Yep. That's what I said. You can't even tell something's missing," Mark added.

"Hey, Syd. We were just going to come over and see if you wanted to get some lunch."

"Uh, sure, I suppose I could use some lunch. I didn't eat any breakfast," I answered.

"Where do you want to go?" Mandy asked.

"Oh, I don't care. Anywhere is good by me," I said.

"How 'bout we go to that little diner down at the bottom of the hill?" Mark suggested.

"Fine by me," I said. "I'll follow you guys. I need to be back by one to meet Evan's friend, Jake, and his girlfriend, Becca."

"Sounds good," Mandy said as we all made our way back into the parking lot.

Sitting at the booth in the tiny diner, I was having a hard time finding something I thought my stomach would tolerate. It was still not happy with much food.

"Well, I think I'm gonna have the 'Logger's Special', Mark said happily.

"Dear God," Mandy said with a laugh. "That's enough food for all of us."

"You best be orderin your own, 'cause I ain't sharin'," he said in his worst pirate voice possible.

We all laughed. "'Sides, I don't have to make weight for at least three weeks. And I'm hungry!"

We all placed our orders and as the waitress gathered our menus and was walking away, Mandy asked, "Do you guys remember when we used to walk down to the little store across the street when we were kids?"

"Yes," I said with exasperation in my voice. "You guys always made us run across the freeway to save time and it was terrifying."

"OK, always so dramatic," Mark said. "None of us even came close to getting hit."

"Please admit that running across both lanes of north and south bound I-5 is incredibly dangerous and stupid," I demanded.

"Perhaps slightly reckless, but stupid is a strong word."

"Says the father of two small children," I added. "Tell me you wouldn't lose your mind if you found out your children were running across the freeway?"

"That's different," he said, growing remarkably serious. With that, Mandy and I laughed.

"So, are you nervous? Tomorrow's the big day," Mark said to change the subject.

"Yeah, I guess so. I'm not really sure what I'm feeling these days. I'm just trying to take it moment by moment and keep my head," I said with a forced smile.

"Syd, I know this has been a huge blow to you, but you gotta know we're here for you," Mark said.

"Yeah," Mandy chimed in. "There isn't anything we wouldn't do for you. Even though you're the youngest, you've sort of been the light and the air and the stabilizer in this family. As much as we acted like we hated it every single day you'd come out of your room with a huge grin and were always just so happy. You always do the right thing, keep your nose clean, roll with whatever's coming down the pike. I think we may have taken that a bit for granted. We, on the other hand have caused our fair share of trouble. What with Mandy here running away and me having to drop off college to get married. Having a kid at nineteen wasn't the best life plan. We've all relied on you to be the steady one."

Just then the waitress came with our food. "Is there anything else I can get for you?"

"No, thank you, this looks great," Mark said.

"OK, well if you need anything, just let me know."

I looked down at my bowl of plain oatmeal and began to stir it. I was trying to gauge what was behind the tightening in my chest.

"Penny for your thoughts?" Mark asked with his mouth full of French toast covered in eggs over easy and a bite of bacon.

I looked up and said, "Thanks for that, it's really sweet. But I just can't figure out why you guys wouldn't tell me the truth."

It hung there for a long minute. They both looked at their food.

I continued. "I mean, you guys knew this the whole time. When the police took us to that crappy hotel and we went to Aunt Marjie's house, when we went to Alaska and Ed was awful to me, when Mom and Ed went to your wrestling match instead of my Christmas concert. Of course they went to your wrestling match. Why would he miss your match? You're his son. I wasn't his. But you guys saw how much that hurt me. And you stood by and said nothing."

I looked back down at my oatmeal and gave it another stir. Mark and Mandy each took another bite of their food. I tried a small bite. It didn't taste like anything.

"You need to put the brown sugar in that," Mark said. Mandy glared at him.

I poured all of the brown sugar that came with it on top of the oatmeal and started stirring it in.

"Listen, Syd," Mark started. "We were just kids too. We didn't know what to do. We were all just surviving. It's like running across the damn freeway. I mean, we joke about it, but you're right. It's a crazy dangerous thing to do, kids or not. We were on our own a lot to do the best we could with a lot of crap that was just handed to us."

"What about when Mandy ran away? Huh? We weren't really just kids anymore then?"

"That was just a horrible time for all of us," Mandy said. "I'm sorry I wasn't thinking of anyone but myself. I was in a crisis myself."

"OK, guys, that's very nice, but you're not really answering me. Did you know this my entire life?"

They just stared at me and looked awkwardly down at their food.

"Great, you won't even admit it. I'm not trying to rub your noses in anything here. I'm not trying to be the victim or be right. I just want someone to be completely honest with me and stop covering their own ass." I could tell they were shocked. Like Mark said, they weren't used to me being the one to demand much of anything from anyone.

"Listen, Syd. Sure, we knew. We were old enough to know what was going on. And we were old enough to remember," Mark finally admitted.

"Thank you," I whispered. "Thank you for just saying so. But why didn't you tell me? And don't say you didn't think I wanted to talk about it. If I hear that one more time, I think I will lose my ever-loving mind."

"Mom told us not to say anything," Mandy said.

"When? At what point did she say, 'Don't tell Syd'?"

"I don't really remember," Mark said. "Honest, it was just something we knew. We didn't always sit around and talk about how to keep it from you."

"Look," Mandy said. "I get that you're upset and confused about all of this. But I think you're looking for more of a conspiracy than actually existed. It wasn't like that. We weren't watching you suffer and standing back and saying, 'oh well, gotta keep the secret'. We were all suffering and trying to survive. It wasn't a great childhood for any of us. I don't want to be too dramatic because there were lots of great times, but let's be honest, John and Ed were terrible to all of us, each in our own ways."

"I guess what we're trying to say is, we're sorry," Mark said. "Listen, with wrestling for the Army, and now for the US Team, I've had the opportunity to work with some counselors. They tell you it's to help you compete at your highest level, visualization, and performance optimization. But a lot of it, for me anyway, has been cleaning out the crap of not having Dad there my whole life and chasing after his approval. Why the hell do you think I wrestle? 'Cause he wrestled. I figured if I was good enough at what he loved, I might just get his attention. Well, I never did, did I? And you know what. I probably never will. I've come to terms with that. But I've learned to accept that has more to do with him than me. And all the hardship I, we, went through as kids — all of it — it has made us who we are. We are strong because of it. And if I can look myself in the mirror and like who I see looking back, then I can't take back any of what made me who I am. If I look in the mirror and don't like who I see, then it's up to me to make that guy someone I do like. I can only change me. I cannot change the past, and I cannot change anyone else."

"Thanks, guys. I appreciate that. I've been praying every day for help to forgive each person. It's been really hard, but that's my only way through this." We sat there for several minutes of silence. Mark kept eating; I kept stirring, but I felt relieved.

"Syd," Mark asked. "What are you gonna do about tomorrow?"

"Uh, I don't know, get married," I joked to relieve a bit of the tension.

"No, I mean, have you thought about who's gonna walk you down the aisle? You had asked Gus to walk you down before all this broke loose. Any thoughts there?" I sat back and thought about it for a long moment, and then it dawned on me. Mom's just leaving the parking lot even when she saw me coming in. She would never do that. Not even under these tense circumstances. Mark and Mandy hanging behind just the two of them to come take me out to lunch. This was a set up. They were doing her bidding, just like they had been my entire life.

Mandy added, "It's just that he needs to know and no one has felt like they could ask you about it."

My head snapped up. "Are you kidding me right now?" I spat. "You are here to do Mom's bidding, aren't you? This is like a repeat of my entire life. It seems like you care about me, but really, she's just manipulated you into keeping up her illusion so she looks good."

"Whoa, hold on there," Mark interrupted. "That's not true at all. We all care about you and we wanted to talk to you about this before the wedding because after the wedding when you get back from Hawaii, we'll both be gone back home to different states and it won't get talked about, besides this question needs to be answered. You said yourself that you completely forgot about it. Do you want this to go down tomorrow at the church?"

"OK, fine," I said coldly. "You're right. It did need to be talked about, and I appreciate you taking the time and having the conversation. I really do." I paused for a minute to re-gather my thoughts. I was still mad, but he had a point. "I think I'll walk myself down the aisle. Thanks again for lunch and for everything. I really do appreciate it." And I got up and left.

I don't recall any of the time between leaving that diner and pulling into our apartment. Just as I parked, I heard Evan's car coming up the driveway. I glanced in the rear-view mirror to see if I looked as bad as I felt. Nope. I was getting very good at hiding the mess going on inside me.

I quickly got out so I could watch them approach and get out. I needed to look as casual as I could; plus, I wanted to get a glimpse of the much heard about Jake and his girlfriend, Becca. I wasn't at all surprised at his lanky, casual demeanor. Even sauntering around the back of Evan's car made it clear he was easy to be around. Of course, I also had to get a glimpse of Becca, Jake's girlfriend, and make sure she wasn't too pretty or too tiny to go sit by a pool with. Of course, she was absolutely stunning.

"Hey," I called when they were heading my direction. "Great timing. I just got back."

"How did decorating go?" Evan asked.

"Great. I overslept and got there as they finished."

"Perfect," Evan said as he came to my side and kissed me quickly. "You need some sleep!"

"Syd, this is Jake and his girlfriend, Becca."

"It's so great to meet you. I've heard so much about you." Moving to shake Jake's hand he surprised me by leaning out with a quick hug and kiss on the cheek.

"Not nearly as much as I've heard about you, I'm sure, but Evan, come on man, she's not homely."

"Jake," Becca scolded with a smack across his shoulder.

"Hey, ouch." Still rubbing his shoulder for effect, Jake introduced Becca. "Sydney, this is my abusive girlfriend, Becca. But don't worry, she probably won't hit you until she's known you for a day at least."

"Nice to meet you. Thanks for coming all the way up here."

"Oh no problem. I've never been to Seattle before. It's beautiful."

"Well, you're getting nice weather. It usually rains a lot in June, but this year has been amazing."

"We'll take it, believe me. I've visited Evan up here before and froze to death."

"Maybe if you put some meat on your bones your skinny butt wouldn't be so cold all the time," Evan teased.

"Hey, college has served me well," Jake answered patting his stomach.

"That's not meat, that's beer."

"Whatever works."

"OK, we're off to bake by the pool."

"Have they seen this pool?" I asked Evan warily.

"No, they have no idea how posh it really is."

Listening to Jake and Evan reminisce about their juvenile delinquent days occupied the afternoon. I expected the same polite jealousies from Becca I'd been fielding from the girls at my sorority and friends from high school, but they weren't there. Not once did she or Jake make the altruistic observation that I was really too young to be getting married, or inquire of my intentions to finish school.

Lying beside the token postage stamp sized pool in my bathing suit also brought concerned scrutiny from Evan. He didn't get a chance to say anything until Jake and Becca went back to the apartment to get changed for the dinner and he said we'd be along in a minute.

"When was the last time you ate?"

"I had some lunch with Mark and Mandy, why?"

"You don't look good."

"Geez, thanks. Just what a girl wants to hear her fiancé say the day before her wedding."

"I mean you obviously aren't eating. How much weight have you lost?"

"I don't know. I don't have a scale, but I'm fine."

"What are you doing?"

"OK, now you're making me mad. I'm doing the best I can. I'm not on some kind of starvation to look good for the wedding thing, OK. My dress doesn't even fit right anymore. I'm under a bit of stress here and it hurts my stomach to eat."

"How long has that been going on?"

"Well, let's see, since I got back from California with my mom. Gee, I wonder?"

"Sydney, come on, I'm not trying to attack you. I'm worried about you," he said as he pulled me to him in a stiff embrace.

"I know, I know. I'm sure things will get much better after the wedding. It's just going to take some time."

"Hey you two," Jake interrupted from the balcony, "the wedding's tomorrow so knock that stuff off. You better get

157

going, I've seen your mom when she's throwing a party and you don't wanna be late."

"We're coming."

I started to pull away from Evan's embrace when he held me tighter. "Let's take a minute and pray. Lord, this is harder than I even thought. We need you to be here and help. Just get Syd through this. I guess that's it, but really, we need help here. Amen."

"Thanks," was all I could muster as we made our way up the hill to our apartment. "I sure like Jake and Becca."

"Yeah, they're great," Evan answered me, but I could tell his mind was on something else.

Chapter Fifteen

A few of the guests arrived early to Evan's mom's, pulling in right behind us. Our only saving grace was that we were ahead of them, if even by a minute, but she was a bit irritated, which wasn't a good way to start off. I gave Evan a knowing look when we entered the kitchen to see a full bar set up across the back counter.

"Just let it be. Everything will be fine."

"I hope so," was all we could squeeze in before people were upon us with hugs and questions. For the most part I let myself get swept up with the excitement of the evening, enjoying all the people's company and being the center of attention like I had never been before and sensed I'd never be again. But I couldn't keep my eye off the bar. It's not that I have a huge problem with alcohol per se, it's just that growing up at the mercy of an alcoholic dad and step dad, it made me incredibly nervous. I had learned to always be on high alert when people are drinking because you never know when they will turn nasty.

But Evan was right, and it really was just fine, until we got to the church for rehearsal and the piano discussion.

I meant to slip out early and get to the church before the throng of people in our wedding party, but once I left, the dinner wound down and everybody followed. That was no problem really, except there were then no less than fifty people standing around the piano discussion offering opinions, which made reaching any kind of solution impossible. Donna was trying to convince us we could put twelve bridesmaids across the stairs and not even know the piano was there; but with all the people in place, they looked like they were right on top of the first row of chairs where my family was sitting.

"Why can't we move the first row of chairs back about ten feet to give more room on the stage?" my mom suggested.

"Because we'd have to take out two rows of chairs in the back all the way across the sanctuary to make it look even and then you wouldn't be able to seat all your guests. You did say you're expecting between four hundred and seventy-five and five hundred people, right?" Donna cautioned.

"Let me see how it looks from the back of the church with all the bridesmaids up there," I offered. But standing in the back of the church didn't make them look any less like a line in the grocery store. Frustrated, I went outside to get some air.

Donna followed me out trying to be comforting, "We'll work this out, Sydney. Don't let it ruin your evening. I promise you we'll be able to find something that…"

"This is not going to work." Karen's angry voice stopped Donna cold, I could hear the gin barbing her every word. I knew that bar would be a problem. "You promised no piano on that stage, and there will not be a piano on that stage."

"I understand you being upset about this, but if we all stay calm, we can solve this."

"I am calm," Karen insisted, her words betraying the alcohol fueling her anger.

"Please, you're shouting at me. We just need to brainstorm this."

"This is not shouting. Now you need to get in there and call whoever you need to call to get that piano moved. We would never have held this wedding here with that piano in the way."

So engrossed in their argument, neither Karen nor Donna noticed me back away and head toward the parking lot. I don't know how I decided upon sitting beside the car or how long it was before Jake found me.

"Hey, what're you doin' out here, your party's in there?" Jake asked gently as he slid down the car to sit on the hot black top beside me.

"I don't know. Karen started into the wedding coordinator, and I needed to get some air I guess."

"Ah don't worry about Karen. Really, I've known her most my life. She sounds like she could rip you apart, but she's harmless."

I smiled at his attempt to cheer me up.

"When me and Evan were kids all of us were a bit afraid of her, but after a while, you knew she had a good heart and just sounds pretty harsh a lot of the time. I remember not wanting to spend the night over there because they never had sugar cereal and to make that worse, she made you drink all the milk out of the bottom of your bowl with the little bark chunks left in it."

The earnestness in his voice made me chuckle.

"Hey are you laughing at me?" he teased, hoping he'd lightened my mood.

"Yeah, I guess I am. You were afraid of her because she made you drink your cereal milk?"

"Are you kidding? That was traumatic for me. I think I still have scars and to this day, mostly I eat cinnamon toast and hot cocoa for breakfast. I bear the scars of it."

At that we both laughed. "I guess we should head back in

there and survey the damage."

"Here, let me help you up."

"Thanks."

We weren't but a few steps back inside the church when the carnage of the argument was clear. Donna was wiping her nose, obviously trying to keep from crying with my mom explaining why it had to be moved, and the piano was down off the stage like we'd planned. Apparently, Karen distracting her with an argument was a part of the plan to move the piano while she was preoccupied.

Scanning the room for Evan, he found me before I found him. As he came closer, I caught the knowing look he exchanged with Jake, but before I could say anything his warm hand was holding my cheek and he gently tucked my head against his shoulder. "Thanks man," he whispered as Jake moved away. Sensing everyone's eyes upon us, Evan kissed the top of my head and teased, "Let's get this show on the road."

On his cue, everyone made their way to the back of the church and out into the lobby to line up in the order they walked down the aisle

Donna had everyone paired up according to the list I'd given her. Evan, Scott and Jake were up front with our pastor, Mike. The candle lighters mapped out their paths with the guys going down the outside isles and the girls the center aisle. They would then light the altar candles together and take their places. One by one the bridesmaids and groomsmen made their way down the aisle on Donna's cue until there were only Justin and Leah in front of me. I stood there holding my three bouquets of ribbons carefully removed from bridal shower packages and expertly arranged on paper plates.

I was so lost in thought, I didn't see Leah coming. Before I knew it, her little arms were around my knees and there was no way I was going to keep my balance. Falling backward with her, I could only think that I didn't want to land on her or land with my dress up. For the first few seconds we were on the ground the entire room was silent. But when I started laughing, everyone did. Sitting in the middle of the aisle with Leah perched on my lap, I tried to gently scold her through my laughter so she wouldn't think she should tackle me during the wedding. Of course, her three-year-old mind had no explanation for the football move in the aisle, so we just got up, sent her back to the front of the church where her mother held her dress so she couldn't repeat the move, and resumed walking the aisle.

When we'd practiced leaving and then entering again — the second time with the seating of the parents, we made our way to Baskin Robbins for some ice cream. Before everyone left, I made sure each person knew they needed to be at the church by three thirty to get dressed, get a wedding party of twenty-eight photographed, and be ready for the seven o'clock wedding.

Unlike the reception hall, I insisted on being a part of the church decorating for the wedding. We couldn't get started until two because there was a noon wedding before us. When the last guest from the first wedding drove away, we furiously transformed the yellow ribbon and candles into a sea of peach. The first order of business was the ribbon adorned, champagne rosebud flower arrangements at the center aisle of each row with sheer peach gauze draped between chairs. Along both the center and outside aisles were ten tier candelabras, each with peach tapirs waiting to make the room glow with the setting sun. We still weren't sure how many times Kari would have to sing 'Doubly Good To You', in order to give the candle lighters time to illuminate seven hundred and fifty candles.

The altar, piano removed, was adorned with four fifteen tapir candelabras lavished with soft peach roses and greenery. Behind the pastor was a table covered with a peach tablecloth layered with more of the sheer gauze from the aisles, and topped with a white lace runner my grandmother knit. Upon the runner was the unity candle with a single candle on each side representing the separate lives Evan and I brought to this wedding. When I was setting them in their places, I chuckled at the straight, pristine wax of my candle. There were no dents, blemishes, or gaping holes that made the candle unable to stand proudly erect in its place. I thought to myself, if the candle can do it, I can.

"Hey, no standing around, we're not quite done and it's already ten past three," my aunt's teasing voice called me out of my daydream.

"I know, I know."

"You need to tell all the girls to be careful with these candles. The gauze netting off the back of their hats could catch fire."

"Come on, how likely is that?"

"I caught on fire in your mother's wedding."

"Get out of here, how?"

"I was the only bridesmaid, so I had to do all the work of holding the flowers, straightening the dress, getting the rings, everything. When I went back to straighten her dress one time, I passed the candles too close and my veil caught on fire."

"Fire, fire or was it just melted a bit?"

"No, fire, fire, the kind with flames. My hair was singed."

"What did you do?"

"I screamed, ripped it off my head, threw it on the ground and stomped the flames out. Then we went on with the ceremony."

"Did you ever think that was an omen?"

"Omen for what?"

"Didn't that marriage pretty much crash and burn?"

"I guess it did. Never thought of it that way." After an awkward pause, my aunt found something to busy herself with, leaving me to wonder why I'd never heard that story before. I had to admit it's pretty funny and I would have laughed if the timing had been different, but I was stuck on the notion that I'd never heard it. My family loves their stories, beats them into the ground with over-telling if they're any good, but this one had never been mentioned. I wondered how manymore untold stories lay hidden in the people swarming around the room as I made my way to the back of the sanctuary to take in the whole room. Satisfied everything was just as I wanted it, I took the white linen runner and carefully rolled it down the length of the aisle, not to be walked upon until the seating of the parents. It really was beautifully decorated and for a moment, I felt like it could be a fairy tale wedding.

"We have your dress ready for you," my sister's voice broke through my trance.

"Is everything else done?"

"Yip, time to get dressed for pictures."

"I really need another shower. I've been sweating like a pig. How hot is it?"

"I heard someone say it's over ninety, but no time or place for a shower. You can take a sponge bath, but your hair's already done, remember?"

"Oh, yeah, I guess you're right."

"You have to close your eyes before you go in the changing room. We have a surprise for you."

"What kind of surprise?"

"Nice try, just close your eyes and I'll lead you."

I could hear a lot of people in the room we entered, all being quiet, of course. "OK," she said stopping me and turning me a little so I was aimed to look at whatever she had before me. "You can open your eyes."

Hanging before me was my dress. Although I'd seen it a hundred times, tried it on dozens of times, somehow this was different. It hung from the ceiling to allow the five-foot train to cascade down and drape along the floor. Sure, it wasn't all that Princess Di's train was, but I loved it. I gasped and covered my mouth, tears forming in my eyes. The ornate lace around the high neck looked suspended in thin air with only the sheer gauze leading to the scoop neckline. Each sleeve billowed at the shoulder before the lace overlaid satin narrowed to a slim line ending in a point to cover the back of my hands. The tiny bodice, laden with beading and lace ornately drew your eye to the hip line, also finishing in a point at the skirt. Hanging loosely without the underskirts, the sheer fabric overlaid the bright white satin. It lay smooth until below the knees were rows of lace met up with the tiered lace filling the train. Beside the dress hung my veil made of matching sheer fabric finished with lace.

"Aren't you gonna put it on?" Lesa's childlike voice broke the frozen moment.

"Yeah, I am," I whispered, looking into her bright eyes. The innocence of a child's mind shined through her adult eyes betraying the disability my childhood friend could not hide from the world if she were aware of it enough to want to hide it.

"Well, let's get this show on the road," she sang out sending everyone into laughter.

It was like a gun went off and all twelve bridesmaids started madly dressing. By the time I had my sponge bath taken, the last possible application of deodorant applied, everyone else was dressed. I felt conspicuous standing in the middle of the room in my strapless, backless bra, white lace underwear and stockings with everyone watching as I donned my two crinoline skirts. Ready for the dress, my sister and sister-in-law carefully lifted it over my head, making sure not to graze my stiffly curled hair or make-up. Once the waist rested on my hips and skirts, I pulled my arms into the sleeves. It took two of them working, but they managed to button each of the forty-five satin covered buttons lining my spine. Completing my dress was the veil. I had to kneel so they could pin it in my hair. With each piece of my wedding dress on, I believed it was real, and a knot of nerves formed in my stomach.

Kris asked, "Do you have something old, something new, something borrowed, something blue, and six pence for your shoe?"

"What, I've never heard the six pence part before?"

"Yep, most haven't, but don't worry, I have one for you." And she held up a tarnished looking coin.

"Won't that give me a blister?"

"Who cares, it's tradition," she answered bending down to put it in my shoe. "Now, let's see, the dress is new, the garter has blue, what did you borrow?"

"These pearl earrings," I answered. "And my pearl

necklace is old. Well, not really old, but I've had them for a few years, and I want to wear them, 'cause they're the only real piece of jewelry I own, they're my favorite, it's the birthstone for June, which is my birthstone, and it's June. So I should be all set."

Standing before the mirror, I didn't really believe it was me looking back. "Will you tell Evan I'm ready to meet him in the sanctuary before pictures begin?" I asked my sister.

I should have known by the look she gave my mom something was up, but I was too lost in my image in the mirror.

"Well, we're running a bit behind, so we just need to get the pictures started."

"I just want him to be alone in the sanctuary the first time I see him today. He's never seen my dress before."

"I know that's what we planned, but he's not here yet and it's already almost four, so we need to get pictures started while we're waiting for him."

"He's not here yet?"

"No."

"Didn't he know he was supposed to be here by three thirty?"

"I think so, but you know Evan, he's always late."

"There's a difference between always being late and showing up late for your own wedding." There was clear irritation in my voice.

"Hey, hey now, you shouldn't be irritated with the groom on your wedding day. That can't be good," my sister tried to joke.

"I know," I snapped. "I guess we'll just get started then." With that I gathered up my skirt and marched up the stairs to the sanctuary.

Distracted by posing for all the pictures needed of just me, with the bridesmaids, my family, the flower girl and ring bearer, the flower girl alone, with the groomsmen, and just about everyone else I'd ever known in my entire life, I lost track of the time. It was past six when I heard Evan's voice in the foyer of the church. No one thought to stop him before he came in the sanctuary. As his gaze met mine, he stopped mid-sentence and stride to take me all in. My only thought was that my moment was ruined. I wanted him to be standing alone at the altar when I came in, just the two of us. But there he stood at the back of the crowded sanctuary still wearing shorts and a tank top and it was me standing at the altar, only surrounded by bridesmaids when he first saw me in my wedding dress.

"You're going to have to let this go. Don't let one disappointment ruin your special day," my sister whispered in my ear.

I broke Evan's gaze to look at her. I knew she was right, but what I really wanted to do was kill him, just then. I mean just a little bit, but kill him a little bit.

Evan dropped his bag and walked across the room to greet me. It had already been made very clear to him how much of a problem it was for him to be so late, and show up not even dressed. The room hushed as he got closer to me. I met his gaze and held it as he approached. When he was close enough, he uttered, every so quietly, "You're more beautiful today than anything in all creation."

"Thanks, you're late today and lucky to be among all creation. What have you been doing?"

I meant to be cutting, but it came out sarcastic and everyone laughed; everyone except Evan and me that is. He just bent to kiss my cheek and when close he whispered, "I'm sorry. I was playing pickle ball with Greg and time got away from me."

"Are you kidding me? Pickle ball? Greg was here at three thirty, and dressed in a tux, no less," I said.

"Yeah, but after he left, I still had to pack and stuff." He apologized with his warm smile and was off to get into his tux so we could finish pictures before the guests started arriving. I just shook my head and glanced around at the rest of the people in the room. No one thought it was amusing.

On my way downstairs to be hidden from the guests until the ceremony, I caught a glimpse of what looked like 300 people waiting outside the church for pictures to finish so they could be seated. I thought how tacky that must seem, but there was no changing it.

"Can you help me pee?"

"Wow, with all that on, I don't know how."

"I can get out of the slips pretty easily, and then we just have to keep my dress out of the toilet."

"Doesn't sound hard, but with the way this day has been going, I'm not sure we should chance it."

With that we both started to giggle and couldn't stop. Finally, we were so loud some of the bridesmaids came in to see what was going on.

"What are you guys doing in here?"

"Well, I have to pee and we were just trying to figure out how to do that without dipping part of my dress in the toilet."

"You don't want that to happen!"

"Yeah, that might push me over the edge, but if I don't go soon, it's going to be too late anyway."

"OK, here, let me untie the slips and then you step out of them."

"Now, if we go in the handicap stall, a bunch of us can hold your dress all the way around you and it won't get in the toilet."

"Don't you think that's going a bit above the call of duty for a bridesmaid?"

"No way, whatever it takes."

"OK, but I'm warning you, I really have to go."

My mom came in to find me perched on the toilet with three people holding my dress up around me.

"Oh my God, you look like a frog on a lily pad."

With that we all burst out laughing again. She had to shout over us so we could hear her, "It's time for you all to get lined up. We're going to begin seating in about five minutes."

"Wow, already? Is everyone here?"

"Just about. The church is pretty packed."

"Oh my gosh, I need to get my slips back on. Hurry."

"Here, you girls go get your flowers and be ready to go, I'll help her with this."

"Aren't you seated before we go in?"

"Yeah, good point, you help her with the slips and I'll go get ready to go in."

With that my mom was off, I flew into my skirts and we were ready.

Just inside the bride's room, I could not believe my ears. Resonating through the ceiling were the far too familiar words, 'Shot through the heart, and you're to blame. Darlin' you give love a bad name'. And the drums and guitar kicked in. In a panic, I rushed out into the hall way to find Scott, Evan's second best man.

"Scott, they're playing the wrong side of the tape. You have to go change it, quick."

As realization took hold of him, he looked at me in amazement, "Is that 'You Give Love A Bad Name'?"

"Yes, and I don't want it played at my wedding. Quick, go tell him to flip the tape."

Scott was off, but didn't catch the sound guy before the first chorus echoed through the church. Leaning with my forehead against the wall, it took all I had to not start pounding it against the hard surface. Eventually, my sister came out and led me by the shoulders away from the wall.

We all grew quiet as the music changed and we knew the candles were being lit. It was time for the bridesmaids to head upstairs to line up.

Before I knew it, I was all by myself. Picking up my bouquet, I was caught by how beautiful the flowers were arranged. The apricot and champagne-colored roses gathered with baby's breath in a dinner plate size circle were interspersed with wispy dark greens. They gradually tapered down to a trail of roses that reached my knees when I held them in place.

Standing at the back of the church lit only by the setting sun through the stained-glass windows and hundreds of candles flickering was overwhelming. Tears gathered in my eyes, but didn't spill over onto my cheeks, but glistened in the candle light. I could feel the flowers trembling in my hands as I started the slow procession. Locking my eyes on Evan's was my stability. I thought to myself, God is good to give me such a moment as this.

Our pastor started the ceremony with, "Please be seated everyone. Welcome to this wonderful occasion celebrating Evan and Sydney's wedding." And then he turned his attention to us. Smiling, he looked at Evan and said, "Nice to see you could make it, Evan, and so nicely dressed for the occasion." Those who knew Evan was so late and showed up in shorts laughed, which made the rest know there was an inside joke they didn't understand and the laughter caught on and soon everyone was laughing. Evan opened his mouth to say something, but the pastor headed him off. "Evan, an important lesson in marriage is knowing when not to speak, and this is your first opportunity." Which rekindled the dying laughter. I glanced away from Evan to our pastor for a moment in an effort to thank him, for the laughter helped ease my nerves and I stopped shaking.

Chapter Sixteen

Finishing school consumed my attention for the next few years. I insulated myself with studying and student teaching to the extent that I graduated a year early, with honors. It was for sure a distraction from the glaring issue staring me in the face, but earning a double degree with honors in three years was easier than sorting through the madness of my mom's revelation. I didn't even allow my parents' dash to Reno to marry each other when I was twenty-one to faze me. A few friends hinted that I should be so happy now that my parents were married to each other, but only Evan saw beneath the smile and façade of coping. On the outside, it looked like it had my entire life. I was good at this. I was thriving, doing well in school, and always had a smile on my face. Inside, I was withering under the pressure of keeping my anger and fear at bay, fears of what I wasn't even sure. Often times I would curl into myself and disappear.

Just three months after graduation, my first daughter, Mia, was born, and a short year and a half later, Skye. When they were only two and seven months old, I was pregnant again. We had not planned any of these pregnancies, and there were plenty of jokes about helping us figure out what was causing them, but safe to say that being a mother to three in three years at only twenty-five was all consuming and incredibly overwhelming.

Sitting down to eat dinner, I told Evan, "My back hurts.

This just might be labor."

"'Bout damn time," Evan joked. "Let's get that guy out here."

Throughout dinner, my backache grew worse. As we were clearing the dishes, Evan said, "I want you to leave these dishes for me when I get home. I mean it, Syd. If your back hurts, you just lay down, but I gotta get to basketball."

"I don't think you should go. My back really hurts."

"Honey," he said slowly. "I really hope, more than anything, it is labor. You're three weeks late for God's sake. But let's be realistic about this. If it is, we'll have a baby sometime next week." He just looked at me — chin lowered with eyebrows raised. He was right. Mia's labor was four days long and required all the Pitocin they could give me. Skye's was three days and also required Pitocin.

"Yeah, you're right. But come home right after, OK."

"Promise," he said with a kiss on the back of my neck as he hustled upstairs to get dressed for basketball.

After he left, I finished up the dishes knowing he'd be irritated, but I hate dishes in the sink, read the girls some stories, and went upstairs to give them a bath. They loved the bath, and played until the water was cold. All the while, my backache grew worse. As I got the girls out of the bath, a pain tightened across my back and stomach at the same time that felt like a Charlie horse that someone was punching. I sucked in a huge breath of air so loud Mia asked, "Mommy, what happen?"

"I think it's time for the baby to come." And I sat down on the bed, held my stomach and tried to breathe until it eased. After about a minute, it lessened, and I started moving quickly to get the girls into their pajamas. I got them all dried off, the tub drained and toys put on the side of the tub to dry. I had Mia's pajamas in hand and was leading her to Skye's room to get hers when the next wave hit me. It started feeling like a burning fist inside me. I tried to keep moving and breathing through it, but had to stop and brace myself against the door jamb. Both girls were in Skye's room waiting for me, so I just stood there, trying to breathe and think at the same time until it passed. Who should I call? The plan is for the girls to go to the neighbor's house, so as soon as I get them dressed, I can call them. Then, I'll call my mom, and she can drive me to the hospital if Evan doesn't get here soon. Sitting on Skye's bed, I got Mia into her nightgown and pull-up before the next fireball came. Breathing with my head down, I waited thinking I should really try to figure out how long between these.

When it eased up, I asked Mia, "Can you please go get the phone off mommy's nightstand and bring it to me? Skye, come here honey, let's get you in your jammies." I helped Skype up on her bed and got her diaper and sleeper on as Mia came back with the phone. "Thanks love, now please go in the bathroom and bring me the hairbrush." I started dialing my neighbor's number and the next wave hit, stronger than the last. I hung up, but not before I heard her voice. She heard me gasp when it hit before I hung up, and guessed what was up. Thank God we had not locked the front door.

Before it even peaked, I heard Cathy's voice calling from the front door, "Syd, it's Cathy. Is everything OK?"

"Hi Caty. We're upstaws," Mia answered.

I heard Cathy climbing the stairs and say to Mia, "Hi Mia, where's your momma?"

"She's in Skye's room. Her tummy huwts and she tinks the baby's comin'. I got the pone and the bwush," Mia said, very proud of herself.

"That's great," Cathy said as she and Mia came into Skye's room.

The contraction was subsiding by then and I smiled at her, sort of. "Thanks so much for coming. Evan's at basketball. Can you call my mom to come and take me to the hospital? I have the number dialed in."

"Sure, how far apart are the, oh hi, Leslie, this is Cathy. I'm over at Syd's house. She's in labor and Evan's at basketball. She needs you to come and take her to the hospital." There was a pause and then Cathy said, "Yes, I'll keep the girls."

Just about then, we heard Evan open the garage door and his car pull in. Quickly, he was at the top of the stairs talking to Mia. "Mommy's in Skye's room and her tummy huwts weal bad. Caty's here to take us to her house. The baby's comin, the baby's comin!"

"Wow, that's exciting."

"Hey, Cathy," he said as he stood in the doorway to Skye's room. "Seems like things have turned up a notch since I left."

"Well, I don't know what they looked like when you left, but you need to get her to the hospital, right away." There was a lot of scolding in her tone.

"Cool. I'll just jump in a quick shower, and we're off."

"Are you kidding me. You are absolutely not taking a shower. I need to go now. I can't even walk!" I insisted.

"Wow, all right then. No shower. Can I at least change?"

"NO! You cannot do anything but help me get in the car and drive me to the hospital."

He opened his mouth to say something, but I cut him off.

"And God help you if you tell me to settle down."

Slightly put out, he made his way from the door to the bed to wrap his arm around me to help me up, when another contraction hit.

"Wait, wait, wait," was all I could get out before I fell back and closed my eyes to try and breathe through it, squeezing his hand harder than I needed to — for effect.

When it subsided, he gently lifted me up and helped me to the car. I could tell it was all he could do not to be a little frustrated by my notoriously low pain tolerance and classically dramatic reactions to pain. After all, this was going nothing like the first two.

On the way to the car, I told the girls, "Isn't this exciting? Momma's going to the hospital to get the baby out of my tummy, and you are going to sleep at Cathy's house."

"Have fun, Momma," Mia cheered.

"Can you let my mom know to just come to the hospital?" I asked Cathy.

"Sure, I'll watch for her car. Good luck!"

I couldn't spare the concentration or energy to pay any attention to Evan as I tried to leave the girls in a settled state. Once in the car, I just closed my eyes and tried to breathe the best I could. Every now and then, I would open them to look at the speedometer. We were on the freeway, but cautiously going 55 mph as if there were not a care in the world. Finally, I semi-hissed, "Can you go faster?"

"I'm hurrying," was all he said.

Just before the next fire ball, which had now built to inferno levels, I felt incredibly nauseous and felt like I was going to throw up. I started looking around for something to throw up into, but found nothing.

"What do you need?"

"I'm gonna throw up, do you have anything?"

"What, you can't throw up? You throw up right before the baby's born, we're still on the freeway. We're not there yet. You can't throw up." I was about to say, you finally believe me, but the explosion in my abdomen and back happened again, and now I was struggling to also keep the spaghetti dinner inside too. Even with my eyes closed and all my concentration on breathing, I did notice that we were suddenly going much, much faster.

Careening to a stop beside the emergency room entrance, Evan said, "You stay here, I'll go get some help."

Within seconds, Evan and two nurses were running toward the car with a gurney. They found me leaning out my open car door throwing up all of my spaghetti dinner.

"We gotta hurry," Evan said. "She only does that right before the baby is born."

They helped me out of the car and onto the gurney, all the while asking rapid fire questions.

"Who is your doctor? Did you call her before coming? Are you pre-admitted? How far apart are the contractions? When is your due date?"

Evan only knew our doctor's name and the due date. In between infernos, I was able to tell them, yes, we're pre-admitted, confirm, the due date was October 6th, three weeks ago, and no, we did not call the doctor yet. The contractions are about one to two minutes apart.

When we got inside the emergency room, the nurses saw all the blood and fluids on my clothes, and made the decision to take me straight to the OB floor. Talking on their radios on the way, they learned the OB floor was full, but an OB nurse would meet them on the medical part of the OB floor and that our doctor was in-route for another patient.

When we got into a room, two nurses were there and one was talking fast, but in a calm voice.

"Hi, my name is Julie, and this is Karen. We will be taking care of you." They lifted me from the gurney to the hospital bed and instantly started cutting off my pants. Karen then started an IV while Julie said, "I can see your baby's head. Don't worry, Sydney, if your doctor doesn't get here, Karen and I can deliver this baby. We've done it a thousand times."

I looked at Evan with panic racing across my face. He knew I was thinking of my Aunt Marjie who died in childbirth. Our girls' births were nothing like this. He stepped close, took my hand and put his face beside mine. "You're fine. Everything's fine. The baby's going to be perfectly fine. We're in great hands here."

"Can you please call an anesthesiologist?" I asked.

Julie looked at me. "I'm sorry, honey. Far too late for that. You're ready to push. Just let us get the basinet ready and we'll get this baby born."

"Why aren't we on the baby floor? This isn't like the rooms our girls were delivered in. It doesn't have all the stuff," Evan asked.

"The hospital is absolutely full with storm babies," Julie explained.

"What are storm babies?"

"You recall about nine months ago when Clinton was being inaugurated? We had that terrible storm, power was out for three days most places. We got a lot babies come out of that. God help us if Seattle ever wins a super bowl!"

"Oh, well, how about that," was all Evan could say.

"These are the medical rooms for patients who are here

but not having babies. But not to worry. We'll take great care of you." Julie was working and talking at the same time.

And then the next inferno hit. It was worse than the previous ones. I bit down, clenching my teeth as hard as I could. I felt the wisdom tooth I had had taken out of my upper jaw when I was fourteen, perfectly intact, roots and all, and transplanted into my lower jaw to replace an adult tooth I was missing, break loose. The transplant never took, so it was only held in place by cement attaching it to the two teeth beside it. I was afraid I would choke on it, so I took it out of my mouth and placed it in Evan's hand. He stared at it for a second and then said, rather shocked, "Uh, she just pulled out her tooth." And he looked up at Julie who was watching the baby's head. "She didn't do that with the first two."

For a few seconds, all three of them, Evan, Karen, and Julie, just stared at my tooth in Evan's hand. I couldn't explain that I didn't actually pull a tooth out of my head because of the inferno. Finally, Julie said, "Oh my God, she's pulling out her teeth, call an anesthesiologist."

I heard Karen talking about the need for an anesthesiologist, stat.

When the inferno subsided and I opened my eyes, my doctor and someone I'd never met before were just walking in. Evan still had my tooth in his hand.

Looking at me, the new doctor said, "Why did you call me, this baby's practically born, you don't need an anesthesiologist."

Julie said, pointing to the tooth, "She pulled out a tooth!"

Evan said, "She didn't do that with the first two."

For a brief second, everyone was looking at Evan, still dressed in a sweaty t-shirt, shorts droopy from sweat, and his knee braces pulled down and still hanging around his ankles. In that brief respite, I was just about to chuckle, but then I felt the next fireball starting.

My doctor asked, "Where are we with the birth?"

Snapping back to the task at hand Julie said, "She's fully dilated, and ready to push. Baby's heartbeat is strong at one hundred and thirty."

Putting on gloves and a gown, my doctor said, "OK, Sydney, I would like you to push with the next contraction, can you do that?"

I just nodded. And it came, the pain, but oddly, relief with the pushing. With one push, Jack was born. Pink, screaming, and healthy.

Dr B, as I called her, gently placed him, covered in thick white paste and blood, blinking at the bright light of life outside my body, on my chest while she cut the cord. She remembered that Evan wanted nothing to do with that after the girls were born. Evan and I stared with wonder at his tiny face. Tears streamed down my cheeks and smeared onto Evan's face so close it was touching mine, as I looked from Jack's face to Evan's. They seemed to be looking at each other for several moments before Jack started instinctively turning his head inward, tiny mouth slightly open.

"Congratulations, Sydney. You did a fantastic job. And I must say you now have the honor of two firsts in my career," Julie said smiling. "Used to be my fastest delivery after arrival was fifteen minutes, but you beat that. You delivered just twelve minutes after arriving. And I've never had anyone pull out a tooth in the middle of labor."

Now that I could talk, I had to explain. "I didn't actually pull my tooth out. I had it transplanted when I was fourteen, but it didn't take so it was just cemented to the teeth beside it. I must have bit down too hard because it broke loose. I didn't want to choke on it." Everyone laughed.

"OK, Sydney, you've got some tearing down here, so I'm going to give you a small shot to numb you before I stitch you up. The shot stings a bit. Have you ever had stitches before?" my doctor said.

"Unfortunately, yes. I'm familiar with the stinging." I pointed to the scar under my chin, which she could see from her vantage point.

"OK, here goes."

More breathing, distracted by Jack's cries as Karen lifted him from my arms to check him over, put ointment on his eyes, and attach his bracelet.

In order to create some much-needed space in the hospital, and because Jack and I were doing so well, we were going to go home the next afternoon. Jack just needed to be circumcised. That didn't happen until about dinnertime, and we were discharged within the hour. The nurse explained that circumcisions bleed some in our discharge instructions, but with two girls, we had no idea what was normal. It was late by the time we got the girls to bed. I fed Jack, changing his diaper between breasts to wake him.

"Evan, I think there's a lot of blood in his diaper."

"What do you expect after what they did to him? He's fine."

Exhausted, I went to bed hoping for a few hours before the next feeding. Mia slept through the night the day she was born, but Skye screamed through the night until she was nine months old, so I didn't know what to expect. Waking to pain in my swollen breasts early the next morning, I thanked God for another good baby. It was well after seven and Jack hadn't woken since I put him down at eleven the night before. Padding quietly to his room so as not to wake the girls, I was shocked to see him in his crib. He lay there blinking awake, but too weak to cry. The blackness of dried blood against the soft green of his crib sheets and blankets sent panic raging through me. I scooped him up to find him saturated in his own blood. I called Evan, who called my mom to come stay with the girls. We were scared, but he ate hungrily and was awake. Evan had called our pediatrician, who was in his office early that morning and said we should bring him right in. I think he had no idea what we were really facing.

"It's his circumcision," I explained to my mom as she came into my room where I was feeding him before we left. "It bled through the night and we think he might need stitches."

"How much did he bleed?"

"Go see his bed, it is really a lot."

When my mom came out of that room she went straight to Evan who was getting us ready to go. "You have to take that baby now, this is not normal."

We went straight to our pediatrician with Jack and all the blankets so they could see what he'd lost. The nurse was impatient at first, explaining that we didn't have an appointment. I looked at her with tears in my eyes. "Please, I think he's lost too much blood," I said as I unwrapped the soaked blankets we brought from home. She froze only for a moment before hurrying us to a room. Within minutes, the doctor was there. I've never known a gentler person than our doctor. He took Jack in his hands and looked to us.

"This baby needs to go to the hospital. Can you take him,

or would you like us to call an ambulance? He'll be fine until you get him there, but are you all right to take him?"

"Yes," Evan answered for us. "We'll get him there."

"Fine, I'll call ahead to Seattle Children's so they'll be waiting for you." Then he looked at me and asked, "Is there any history of bleeding problems in your family?"

"No," I said, not really sure what he meant by a bleeding disorder.

After wrapping Jack's penis in a tight bandage that we decided Evan was in the best shape to hold pressure on in the back seat of the car, we were on our way. Traffic was heavy going into Seattle at that time of the morning, but I honked and weaved in and out of the carpool lane trying to go as fast as possible. We couldn't talk under the weight of our fears. I dropped Evan and Jack at the door of the emergency room while I went to park the car. By the time I arrived inside the hospital, I was dizzy with fear.

"Do you know where my baby is? My husband just brought him in here."

"Does he have the bleeding circ?"

"Yes, that's him."

"Right this way, Mrs. Hood, I'll show you to his room." She took me around the shoulders so kindly. The room she led me to was full. I couldn't see Jack on the bed for all the white coats filling the room, and I caught only a glimpse of Evan's head talking to who I prayed was a doctor.

"Excuse me, I have the mother here, please let us through." The nurse's voice cut through the curiosity and banter. The heads that filled the room turned to reveal young medical students eager to get in on a rare diagnosis. Seeing me there, white with fear, weak from delivering the day before, changed their expressions. They realized this was a family before them, not a case study.

As I moved toward Evan, I could finally see Jack. It was as if I was entering a tunnel that kept growing and I couldn't get to him. He was naked, on his back, with each of his test tube sized limbs tied to the bed. His whole body was bright pink from screaming. The wetness at my breasts made me realize it was Jack's cries I was hearing. A nurse was just putting the final pieces of tape on his IV, the first of thousands that would scar his arms.

"Give me my baby." My voice broke the conversation Evan was having with the doctor. He was a urologist who thought he knew just how to secure that wound. Their heads looked at me and then at my helpless baby strapped down, scared, on that bed. The doctor had replaced our pediatrician's bandage with what looked like a cast on his penis, but the blood was already starting to seep through. The nurse unstrapped him and gave him to me. I wrapped him and held him to me, making my way to the rocking chair to feed him. Consumed with comforting my tiny baby, I didn't notice as the room slowly emptied of all the medical students, the nurses, and eventually the arrogant urologist who scoffed at the idea our pediatrician sent ahead that there was a bleeding problem at work in this case, something out of his expertise. Evan's voice broke my trance,

"They took some blood before you got here. The tests will take a while before they know what's wrong."

"What do they think is wrong?"

"Someone said, Dr Newman wants them to test for hemophilia. He told them that when he called ahead for us."

"I know what that is, but kids with that die of AIDS."

"What the hell, Syd? He doesn't have AIDS."

"There's been a story in the news for months about a little boy in Florida who has hemophilia and he got AIDS from his medicine. They won't even let him go to school. People get AIDS from blood, you know. It's not just gay men and drug addicts."

"He's not going to die." Evan's words were so clear and confident they were enough to let me slip back into my trance. We sat and rocked for the next hours while we waited for the tests. Evan left to get us lunch, but I couldn't touch the tuna salad he brought me from the cafeteria. Worry filled his voice as he urged me, "Sydney, you have to eat to get through this. You just delivered a baby and now you're nursing him."

"I'll be fine as long as I keep drinking, but I can't eat."

Knowing I was resigned, Evan gave up and pushed the food aside.

"Here, you need to hold him while I try to find a bathroom. I didn't bring any pads with me and I'm bleeding like crazy."

"Well, this is a hospital, they should have something for you. I'll ask the nurse."

When Evan and the nurse returned, I mistook their concern for me, thinking it was for Jack.

"What is it?" Panic filled my voice.

"Nothing dear," the nurse assured me, "it's just that we're a children's hospital and don't have adult supplies for your bleeding here in the ER. I'll call the adolescent floor and see if they have pads I can get for you. But you need to keep up your strength. Perhaps some lunch would help."

I looked at Evan knowing he'd put the nurse up to prodding me to eat. He wouldn't meet my eyes.

"I'm really not hungry. But if you could get the pads for me, that would be great."

"Sweetheart, you don't look good at all. I want you to go for a little walk, maybe get some fresh air or something. You can't sit in this room feeding your fears like this. He'll be OK, we just need to find out what's causing his excessive bleeding before we make a treatment plan, but he'll be OK."

With the odd combination of strength and subtlety that makes gravity so amazing, her gentle voice pulled me to her words. She thought my baby would be OK after all the blood in his crib, Dr Newman's obvious concern, and the room full of doctors when I walked in. I didn't know if I wanted to hug her for her comfort, or slap her face for her naïve words in the middle of my torment. In the hours of silence, we'd sat cramped in the only infant room in the emergency room, that was under renovation at the time. Evan had assured himself that Jack was going to be fine and I'd planned his tortured life tainted by the horror of AIDS and ending in a small casket. But I let her gently lift Jack from my arms and give him to Evan. She then took me by the arm and helped me to my feet. With her arm around my shoulders, she led me out of the room.

"Come on, honey, we'll walk up to the patient floors together and get those pads." I followed her, looking back to see Evan settle into the rocking chair quietly whispering something to Jack I couldn't hear. The pain of the ten stitches I needed after giving birth so quickly slowly brought me to an awareness of my own body. For the first time, I took in the brightly painted walls adorned with frogs and birds transitioning to butterflies, airplanes, and trains. We rode an elevator to a floor where the nurse left me to talk in hushed tones with other nurses about my needs. She emerged from a hallway with a bag for me.

"Here are some pads, dear. Why don't you go into the family bathroom and take some time to take care of yourself. There is a shower and linens in there. The hot shower will be really good for your stitches. When you're done, just ask for directions back to the ER."

"Thank you. I won't be long."

"You take the time you need," and she left, walking down the hallway we'd come from as if the world wasn't still spinning.

The stares of those in the waiting room near the family bathroom were full of pity and understanding. I realized the people here know what it is to have something wrong with your baby. They knew the utterly helpless feeling and the raw fear that comes from knowing you can't help him and all your love won't make it better. When I caught my glimpse in the mirror, I understood my frailty. Evidence of the trance I'd retreated into screamed at me from behind swollen eyes and blotched cheeks. Vacillating between chastising myself for the complete weakness with which I'd handled this day so far and a sense that the strength I needed lay within all I knew of God's love, I had a decision to make. I could be the helpless victim of some cruel circumstance, or I could rely on the only true love I'd known since I was four years old and become an active advocate for my child.

Sitting gingerly on the toilet I had to fight to keep breathing as the sight of too much blood brought me back to Jack's crib that morning that seemed like days ago rather than hours. Tending to my own needs kept me in the reality of the situation and restrained me from retreating back to the respite of my trance. I knew at that moment too much blood was going to be a part of my life forever, and I would have to handle it.

The stitches kept my pace slow as I made my way back to the ER. Throughout the halls, I passed families in every state between coping and despair. I was seeing pain in people's faces I'd never had to confront before. What I saw on those strangers' faces prepared me for the complete disbelief storming across Evan's face as I rounded the corner to Jack's room. The doctor's back was to me, but my footsteps interrupted her explanation of what hemophilia is and what it would mean for Jack and our family. Evan looked up and uttered through complete dismay, "You were right, he has hemophilia. His blood doesn't clot right."

Sensing his inability to say anymore, the doctor began at the beginning of her explanation of what hemophilia is and how Jack's blood had performed in the clotting assays. Normal blood takes under five seconds to clot and after thirty-five seconds, Jack's hadn't been able to. It would take days to get back the results that told us how much of the protein called Factor VIII that Jack's blood was missing, but clearly it didn't have enough.

"Will my baby die of AIDS?" I managed to ask with the little breath I could force my lungs to take in.

"No, many hemophiliacs contracted AIDS through the medication they need because it came from the blood supply. But in the last six months the FDA approved a synthetic medication that doesn't come from the blood supply, so your baby won't be exposed to any blood borne viruses. We've called the Puget Sound Blood Center and they are sending some of that medication over for Jack in a taxi as we speak. We'll get that in his system and his circumcision will begin to heal."

"How do you give it to him?"

"It has to go in his IV. We're going to give him his first dose here, then admit him to the patient floor."

"How long will he have to stay?" Evan's voice broke back into the conversation.

"I don't know for sure, but my best guess is several days until his hematocrit is back up and his circumcision is completely clotted and healing."

"What do you mean about his hematocrit?"

"He lost a lot of blood. We're still deciding if he needs a transfusion."

"No. I don't want him to have a transfusion." My own voice sounded foreign in my ears. "If it means he won't make it, then OK, but if it means he just may take longer to recover, I don't want it."

"I assure you, it is completely safe. The blood is screened and tested for the HIV virus and for hepatitis and it goes through purification processes."

"That's all fine and good, but I don't want him to have one if it isn't absolutely necessary. I'm sure that's what that little boy in Florida's parents thought too."

Evan just glared at me.

"OK, we'll consider that when bringing our recommendation to you."

"Will he grow and learn like healthy kids?"

"Yes, hemophilia won't affect his intellect at all, that is unless he has a brain bleed, but those are rare unless he hits his head and you don't get him medicine in time. It may have some effects on his physical body, but all the ramifications of that vary dramatically depending on the child. There are nurses at the Blood Center who specialize in hemophilia care. When we called, they assured one of them will be over when you're ready, to go over everything with you. Also, it's fortunate this is a Thursday. Every Thursday there is a clinic in hematology for hemophiliacs and the pediatrician who specializes in hemophilia is here this afternoon. She said she'd come down and meet with you after her last appointment of the day, which should be within the hour. She'll be able to answer your questions much better than I can."

"Jack's blood failed the clotting tests," I heard Evan whispering to himself as if to make his brain comprehend. "He is a hemophiliac, which means his blood is missing one of the proteins needed to clot blood after an injury."

"Thank you," I said. She smiled and quietly left knowing we needed time together. Some of what she said terrified us. Some sounded OK, I guess. Evan held me, Jack in my arms. We cried quietly. I whispered to Evan out of rote muscle memory from the way I'd reacted to every trauma I'd experienced in my life, "God loves us, I just know it."

"I know He does, I know. Of course, that's true, but not now, OK Syd. Just not now." I sensed some anger and a whole lot of bewilderment in his words. We left each other to our own thoughts.

Within the hour, Dr Mathers appeared in our tiny room. She was a straightforward woman who sat right down and dove right in. "Hello, my name is Diana Mathers, and I'm the pediatric hematologist here in Seattle who treats kiddos with hemophilia. This must be Jack," she said jiggling Jack's toes.

"Yes, this is Jack," I said. "I'm Sydney and this is my husband Evan." Evan stuck his hand out and was about to say something, but she just kept going.

"Well, I know this is quite a shock. Hemophilia tends to

run in families, and for those folks, it's not such a surprise, but for you folks, it's new. Let me give you a brief explanation of what you're dealing with and try to answer your questions. There are thirteen proteins, or factors, that line up in a crisscross fashion like a woven web that clot your blood whenever you break a blood vessel — internally and externally, if it's deep. Your little guy here is missing number 8, which we call hemophilia A. Cuts, like his circumcision, are easy because you can see them and know when they're bleeding and when they're stopping. It's internal bleeding that's more problematic for someone who doesn't clot. But most babies don't hurt themselves, so you have a long while to get your minds around this before you really have to start worrying about it. Really, until he starts walking. That's where the medication comes in. We now have a synthetic medication that doesn't come from the blood supply that will replace only the one factor he's missing and make his blood function normally, but it has a half-life of twelve hours. That means it'll be half gone in twelve hours, and virtually all gone in about thirty-six hours. Have the nurses given him his first dose for his circ yet?

"Yes, they just finished before you came in."

"Great. Now, the really great thing is, we have a wonderful camp every summer for kids and their families, siblings, everyone. They get to spend an entire week with kids just like them, running, swimming, just being kids and it's really well run. There is a full medical staff, so it's perfectly safe."

"Can you go back to the safety of this new medication please?" I asked. "I'm most concerned about the transfer of viruses as I've seen so much in the news about kids with hemophilia who have been restricted from attending school and died from HIV and AIDS they contracted from their medication."

"Yeah, that was a very sad chapter in hemophilia care, but this new medication only has albumin in it, which is one component of human blood, but it can be heated to a very high temperature to purify it and has never contracted anything, so it's a tremendous advancement in hemophilia care. But you will see kids at camp who have contracted hepatitis and HIV from their medication because synthetic medication is only five or six months approved."

"What does this mean for his long term physical and mental health?" Evan asked.

"Hemophilia can lead to some joint damage due to repeated bleeding into the joints, but if you guys are vigilant with the medication and keep him strong and healthy, he can grow up healthy. Hemophilia shouldn't affect his intellect at all. You'll see when you come to camp. Kids running everywhere. I think it'll really put your minds at ease."

I sensed Evan was getting irritated, but then he spoke up. "I'm sure we'll go to camp, probably every year. Hell, we'll probably be camp counselors. In fact, if I know my wife, she'll be Camp Director before Jack's 10, but right now, I don't want to hear about camp. I want to hear about this disease and what it will mean for my son's life."

Unfazed by his outburst, Dr Mathers continued on. "What will really determine what your son's life will be like is how severe his hemophilia is. That will take a few days, but some patients are severe, which means they have zero measurable factor 8, and subsequently ability to clot. Some patients are moderate, which means they have 1 to 3% factor circulating in their blood, which gives them some small ability to clot. Other patients are mild, which means they have 5 to 15% factor circulating in their blood, which means they're usually pretty good except for an injury. There's a gray area between 15 and about 35%, which is what most carriers have."

"What do you think Jack has?"

"It's hard to guess, but given the length of time he has continued to bleed and his assay, I'd say he's either moderate or severe. People with hemophilia do not bleed easier than anyone else, they just bleed longer."

"What do you mean by carrier?" I asked.

"Hemophilia is a genetic disease carried on the X chromosome. Most of the time, women carry the disease, which means one of their X chromosomes have the genetic defect, but their other X is healthy and covers them. Males express the disease because they only have one X, so if it has the genetic defect, they have the disease. The severity of the hemophilia depends on the nature of the genetic defect."

"Can they find that?"

"Yes, most of the time. The nurses from the Puget Sound Blood Center can explain all your options for genetic testing and possibly finding the source of Jack's defect. It might be new with him, or new with you," she said casually, pointing at me.

Unaware of what that casual gesture meant, she talked on about different kinds of bleeds and how soon we could learn to start an IV and treat Jack at home, but I didn't really hear her. I was lost in a circular loop in my mind, of knowing somehow I'd been the source of this, and wondered how I would ever be able to explain that to him such that he wouldn't hate me. The little girl who felt like everyone eventually found a reason to cast her aside started to quake inside me.

I don't know how Dr Mathers ended the conversation, but I mechanically stood and thanked her with a handshake when she left. The nurse who came in to take us to Jack's room on the patient floor where he'd stay until his hematocrit came up and his penis was completely clotted and healed, was right behind her. That turned out to be five days. Once we were settled in our room with three other babies with various problems, Evan went home and got me some clothes, and I settled in. We decided it was best for him to be home with the girls so they weren't too displaced, and I would stay at the hospital with Jack. I was, after all, the only one who could feed him, and he needed all the strength and nutrition he could get to regain his strength.

Curled in the corner of the darkened room on the foldout vinyl chair, on day three, I started to quietly weep. It started with slow tears seeping out the corners of my eyes, but they got away from me, and before long, I had drenched the pillow with snot and tears, my chest was spasming, and the nurse came over to check on me. She tried to sit me up, got me some tissues, and water, but I could not stop crying. Eventually, she called Evan and told him that I needed some company. Our neighbor took the girls again, and he came as fast as he could get there. When he walked in an hour later, tears were still streaming down my face, but I was calmer, with an occasional quiver and gasp wracking my body. He just slid into the pink vinyl chair barely wide enough for one person, tucked me in his arms, and nestled my head into the crook of his neck. It was there where my college roommate, Kris, found us. She stopped by for some lunch and a quick visit with her newborn. Evan insisted we go to at least the hospital cafeteria for some food and a change of scenery. As much as I tried to tell her she shouldn't stay with a little baby, that there were so many germs in the hospital and he could get sick, I was so grateful for her calm presence and warm smile. She was the only person who visited us the entire time we were in the hospital. I wonder if people were afraid, or didn't know what to say.

When we finally went home, it was Halloween day, and I was grateful I had already sewn the girls matching Dalmatian costumes, purchased candy for the neighborhood kids, and could try to make it seem like we were having a fun time, like all the other families with little kids in costumes.

Chapter Seventeen

I took the phone call in the middle of madness. Three-year-old and twice completely potty-trained Mia, was telling me she had a little poop in her puppy panties. Skye, with one arm casted and strapped to her body because I dislocated her elbow while trying to lift her into her car seat by the wrist with one hand while holding Jack, floated her sandwich in her milk while Jack's swing, sure to wake him, slowed to a stop.

"Hi Sydney, this is Barbara from the Blood Center."

"Hi Barbara," I said between looks of instruction and whispers of warning. I had the phone balanced between my ear and shoulder while I tried to wind the swing without waking Jack.

"Dr Thomas has found the mutation. You remember I explained the most common mutations that cause hemophilia? Well, you have one of them, the inversion. Half your factor eight gene is turned around so the sequence reads 23 to 1 and then 24 to 46 instead of 1 to 46."

"Does that mean I am a carrier and I passed hemophilia to Jack?" The chaos in the kitchen faded to nothing as I entered the horrors of my imagination the previous months of waiting afforded me.

"Yes, it does. Dr Thomas has also identified the markers on your gene that he has been able to trace to your parents. It's like the gene has an address like a house number and color that distinguish it from other genes. The mutated gene Jack has causing his hemophilia, you also have. It is the same gene your father has, only it is healthy in him. He, as you know, doesn't have hemophilia. His gene is lined up correctly."

"What does that mean?"

"It means that when the sperm and egg came together at your conception and the genes lined up, for some reason nobody understands, yours changed."

"Oh." I was quiet.

"Are you all right? Does that make sense to you?"

"Yeah, I'm OK. I understand. I've read the stuff you sent me. I understand. Thank you."

"You're welcome, and Sydney, when you're ready, it doesn't have to be for years, but we can test the girls to see if they have the gene as well."

"I'll talk with Evan about that and let you know."

"Whenever you're ready. And if you have any questions, please call. I'd be happy to answer them for you. I can even come out and sit down with you and Evan together if you need."

"Thank you, I appreciate that."

"Bye."

I don't know how long I stood in the laundry room before the crying and chaos pulled me back to the kitchen. It wasn't until that night when Jack's hungry cries plowed into my dreams and I felt the yoke of motherhood drag me from protective sleep, that I faced what I learned that day. I hadn't even told Evan yet. Somehow, this was my news that I kept private. With only the moonlight through the window, I rocked him back to sleep. My breathing kept time with his methodic sucking. I felt as if he could drain my soul right through my breast and hoped it might be enough to get him through whatever his diseased life might bring him. Moving back and forth in the rocker danced the light across his silken hair like a bow across a violin.

When the tiny muscles in his cheeks stopped, I drew him to my shoulder. The fear of losing more sleep to a stubborn burp was swallowed in my sense that I wasn't going to sleep anyway, so I patted his back gently and looked to the heavens. The clouds were dark black in the distance making the moonlight glow above me. I don't know if I was praying or just confirming in my own heart by speaking the words, but I whispered them to the night.

"I should have never been. I was conceived in an affair, ruined both my parents' lives, and was covered over with a lie. Right down to my DNA, I am just wrong. And now my baby, you have to live and die the pain of it. I am so sorry. I am just so sorry."

My eyes had dried, my chest in quiet rhythm with Jack's, and I rocked. The stillness of that night brought my deepest despair; my loneliness left me so hollow only the Lord's voice could touch it. My soul heard him say, "You are my child. I knit you together for my perfect purpose. Don't apologize for my work. What Jack has from you is a gift. Show him my love and trust in my plan." I closed my eyes and slept in the rocker with Jack on my chest.

Knowing how fiercely I'd cling to my hurts, the Lord gave me a picture that night that doesn't need Joseph in his brightly colored coat to interpret. I've never dreamed in such vivid color and detail before or since.

I was a salmon, black and silver on the top of my sleek back. Red tones, that only nature can paint in the fall, adorned my sides and blended into my light silver belly. I saw the journey I'd taken, beginning with the small stream where I grew from an egg to a fry before making my way out to the vast sea. The waters were cold and hard gray, but I navigated gracefully. There were other fish around me, but I was swimming faster, with a determination they seemed to lack. Bits of green lingered at the mercy of the water, so still as I made my way through the darkness. I was aware of predators, but not concerned, confident in my grace and speed. I possessed a sense of purpose fueled by accomplishment. My senses registered everything around me, confirming my deftness: the crabs below me had to side step because they couldn't face what was coming; the large whales only consumed tiny plants, schools of fish darted together for protection they couldn't provide for themselves. All I saw was somehow inferior to my dexterity and the grace of my silent pursuit; yet I didn't feel pompous in my comparison, rather capable.

Suddenly, I was caught in something I didn't recognize. It was webbed and surrounded me so quickly I couldn't react. I realized I'd seen it before, floating along, but I never anticipated it closing in on me, restricting me, holding me in panicked bondage. As the top drew together the hard webbing pushed me to the center, scraping off my beautiful scales, full of protective color. It was pulling me from everything I knew. Gasping for the oxygen in the water, my gills contracted in the dry air. Abruptly, the net dropped, and I lay on a hard surface, unable to maneuver and dive. My fins struggled to glide, but I could only flop spastically. Surrounded by bottom fish, long discarded beer bottles, two, now fast, side-stepping crabs, and dozens of smaller, less skilled fish, I could only struggle to flounder as my muscles seized from their lack of oxygen. But struggle I did until I made my way across the slippery deck, avoiding quick feet and the deadly blow of the club. There was a hole in the side of the ship threaded with a large rope. It was my only hope for making it back to the vast ocean leading to the quiet stream I emerged from where I could spawn, passing on my gift of life. The closer I got, the more I knew I'd make it. Each flop was painful, my body barely clinging to the desire to live. Rubbing against the rope took off more of my beautiful color, but I was still intact as I fell into the icy sea water.

The first gulps of oxygen through my gills restored my strength. Lacking some security in my own ability, but armed with my determination and a sense that I made it back for a chosen purpose, I dove and turned, darting constantly. I knew I'd lost a lot of my protective coloring on the deck of that ship and on the rope that made my survival possible, so I relied more on my surroundings and trusted in my purpose. I was going to my home to spawn for a future my body would be left only to nourish. But I wasn't concerned with what was missing from my body; I was renewed for what my soul learned on the well-worn deck of that fishing boat where many like me lost their lives.

Jack stirred in my arms, pulling me from my dream back to the reality of the cold February night. Gently returning him to his crib, I covered him with the warmth of his blankets. With a peace I wish I could keep a firm hold on, I slipped back into bed and nestled into the heat of Evan's side. As I drifted off to sleep, I thought, I'm gonna need to talk to my parents about this. I can't ignore it anymore, or it will eat me alive.

Chapter Eighteen

Before I lost my nerve, I called my mom early the next morning. Perhaps too early, and I was met with a groggy, "Hello."

"Hey Mom, I'm sorry it's so early. I can tell you're not up yet."

"No, it's fine honey. Is everything all right? Is Jack OK?"

"Yes, he's fine. But the nurse from The Blood Center did call yesterday. The genetic tests are back."

"Oh, that's great. What did they find?"

Trying not to be irritated at her 'that's great' comment, I pressed on. "Well, I guess it's good to know, but I don't know if I'd call it great. Jack's hemophilia definitely came from me."

"But you don't have hemophilia."

"Yes, I know. Remember, I explained this to you? Girls don't have it, they carry it."

"Oh, yes, sorry."

"So, how did that happen?"

"Well, they can positively determine that at my conception, the gene I got from Gus mutated and is defective in me. Gus's gene is healthy, otherwise he'd have hemophilia, and it changed in me."

"But Gus doesn't have hemophilia."

"Yes, I know." I was beginning to get irritated and really struggling to keep it from my voice. "Like I said, it's healthy in him, and defective in me, which makes me a carrier because

I also don't have hemophilia. But because Jack only has one X chromosome because he's a boy and I have two because I'm a girl, I'm a carrier and he has the disease."

"Oh, honey, I'm so sorry. What about the girls? Are they carriers?"

"Yeah, well we'll have to have them tested. They both have a 50/50 chance. That's the way the genetics work with this." There was a pause where neither of us knew what to say. "Anyway, in the little bit of time I've had to process this, it has really made me want to finally address the whole thing — starting with Gus is my father and what happened for him to disappear from my life, all of it. We've brushed it aside long enough, and I can't do that anymore. I need to figure it out."

"Of course, honey. You can come down whenever you want and we'll answer any questions you have."

"You know, I don't think I can swing that, two on one. I don't know what your day looks like, but if you have time, can you come over during the girls' nap time? Then, I think I'd like to talk to Gus on my own. Do you think he'd be willing to have dinner with me tonight? Maybe at that little Chinese place in the Albertson's parking lot?"

"I can come today, and yes, I'm sure he will. What time?"

"They nap right after lunch about one, and let's say five thirty for dinner, that way I'll be home in time to feed Jack before bed."

"Of course, I'll see you at one and he'll be there."

"OK. Thanks. Bye." And I hung up as I heard her say bye.

It was a busy morning, like every morning in our house. It took until nine thirty to get everyone fed and dressed before I could shower and get dressed myself. That is if everything went smoothly. Skye and Mia were playing with the Legos on the floor in my room, Jack was sleeping in his car seat on the floor of my bathroom, and I grabbed a quick shower. It was the only time I'd had to give any thought to what I was going to say to my mom. Really, I wanted to make sure she knew I wasn't angry with her, but I needed to know a few important things. Why did she let a young child make the decision to just not talk about something so important as who her father is? Was my memory of attaching myself to Ed really accurate and did everyone just go along with it? Why did she send me to Alaska? Was that the plan all along or do I remember correctly some last-minute shuffling at the airport? She must have known that would be just awful for me. And what about John? Why did she stand by and let him abuse us day after day? Maybe the last question, why did she let so many years go by with Gus back in our lives before she told me? I should probably write these down. I realized there's a reason why I have put this off until now. She used to joke about how compliant my personality is and that when I was little and one of my cousins got in trouble for something in the living room, I wouldn't even go in that room for fear of getting in trouble. I was very good at learning from watching others. Mandy pushed back and questioned while we were growing up, and it looked like she got sent away to live with her dad. And she all but said it, "Where will Syd go, she doesn't have one of those." That thought brought tears to my eyes and I was thankful I was in the shower to wash them away. I whispered a prayer to myself. I was going to need strength I didn't think I had to get through this. And then I remembered my dream. This seemed like where I would lose some of my scales, but I would make it.

Even though it was February, it was sunny and warm

enough to get outside for some fresh air, so we spent the late morning at the park playing. I was grateful the kids all got some fresh air because it would help with a good long nap that I needed them to take. I'd just finished tucking Mia into her bed with her Ernie doll and was walking down the stairs when I heard my mom's car in the driveway. I checked my watch, twelve fifty, early as always. I took a deep breath and hustled to open the front door so Mia wouldn't hear a knock or ring, and hoped she didn't hear the car. If she had, there would be no nap, especially if she knew it was Grandma. I wish she thought of these things when she decided to show up ten minutes early!

Opening the door just as she reached the front porch, I whispered, "Hey Mom, I'm glad I caught you before you knocked or rang the bell. I don't want the girls to realize you're here. They just went down."

"Oh, I came a bit early hoping I could see them before they went to sleep," she whispered back obviously disappointed.

"Nope, they would never go down if they knew you were here."

"Oh, I didn't think of that."

"Well, come on in." And I moved aside to let her go by me. I followed her into the kitchen and asked, "Do you want something to drink?"

"Just some water would be fine."

"Sure." She was starting to sit at the table still littered with lunch, so I suggested,

"Why don't we sit over on the couch? That way we don't have to deal with the lunch disaster."

"Here, let me clean this up for you."

"No, Mom. You didn't come to do my dishes. Let's just sit on the couch. The dishes aren't going anywhere but who knows how long the girls will sleep," I said, getting two glasses of water. She was making her way over to the couch and stopped to gaze at Jack who was laying on his blanket asleep.

Joining her, I handed her a glass and sat down with my notes in hand.

"You have notes?" she asked nervously.

"I didn't want to lose track of my thoughts," I said.

"Can I ask you why you've let all this time go by without bringing this up at all and then now, out of the blue, you just sort of blind side me with it?" There was accusation and victimization in her tone.

"I don't think I had the courage until now. Believe me, I've given it a lot of thought over the last four years, and it's been gnawing at me. I have asked myself the same question many times. Evan has asked me countless times. But I just didn't have the emotional bandwidth.

"I think I may have realized this morning. You know how you've always joked how when I was little I wouldn't even go in a room where Jeff or Greg got in trouble and that I was very good at learning from watching others get in trouble?"

"What does that have to do with anything?"

"Well, growing up, I've watched Mandy, and sometimes Mark, get into what looked like big trouble for pushing back with you. It looked to me from my young, naïve perspective that Mandy got sent away, and I remember the summer after Mark graduated and he kept doing things you didn't like, you unloaded on him the likes of which I'd never seen. I learned never to push back or cross you. I've lost just about everyone, for sure every parent, three dads, even if they were terrible dads, they were still the only dads I knew, and I lost them. I don't think I could bear the thought of losing you."

"That's ridiculous. I have never left you and I never will."

"I know that, but you did leave them in one way or another and I've never risked it by pushing back — except once. I pushed back in the tiniest of ways and you slapped me right across the face. So, that's why I think I've let four years go by without ever talking with you about this.

"But these genetic tests pointing to me and my conception, they're too much for me to stuff down. I can't do that anymore. It will eat me alive. So, I'd like to ask you some questions.

"Fine, ask away," she said with great effort to control her emotions. I couldn't discern just what emotions: anger, shame, bitterness, so I forged ahead.

"Why did you put Ed's name on my birth certificate to begin with?"

"Oh, that wasn't even my idea. It was Ed's." I could her relax a little to be able to assign this to someone else as if she didn't realize she was still the responsible party. "He had your brother and sister for the weekend just before you were born and when he brought them back, he asked me if Gus was going to do the right thing by me. I said I didn't know. It was then he said, 'you should just name that baby Rossler and raise them all the same. It won't be any good for one of them to be different in the same house'. When I told Gus about it, he thought it was a great idea. Probably 'cause it let him off the hook, and that made me mad. But it was also the best thing for you. His family would never have accepted us and you would have always felt like an outsider, so what I did was for the best.

Look at them now, Iris' kids are all screwed up, George's kids have never even left home as adults. I didn't want that for you."

"How could you have known any of that then?"

She just stared at her water for a long minute and then repeated with barbs in her words, "They would not have been good for you at all. I did what I thought was best and I was right."

I took a deep breath and decided to move on. If I wanted answers to my questions, I was not going to be able to debate with her. "I remember you said I knew Gus as my dad until I was five and then I decided not to talk about it anymore. Why would you let a child make a decision that important?"

She took a long, deep breath, and then another one. "I did what I believed was best for you. You were too young to understand the court trial and why Gus couldn't come around anymore, so I just let it go. I could have made up lies, but it seemed better to just let it go."

"Aunt Marjie told us Gus was sick and that's why we couldn't see him anymore."

"That wasn't a lie."

"I realize that, but he wasn't sick forever. We saw him with Nick and Christine after I got my stitches when I was nine. So at some point, he got better and he could have re-entered my life as my dad."

"He tried to kill John. John didn't want him around."

"So you chose John as my dad over Gus as my dad. You made that choice for me?"

She didn't answer. "I thought John could provide for us the childhood I had before my dad died. We used to go camping and fishing and hunting. John loved to do all those things. I thought he could provide all those things for us that I had as a child before my dad died. When I was in sixth grade, I came home from school on my birthday and I couldn't go in the house because my Grandpa King had died in our house and I had to wait outside until the coroner came and took his body away. Then, the next year, on my birthday, my uncle died on my birthday. Had to cancel my birthday party again. Then, the next year, when I was in eighth grade, at least not on my birthday, but that year, my dad died. I lost everyone. You remember when Margaret died. I've just lost so much. I thought John could bring back some of what I had before my dad died." She was talking through thick emotion and tears were streaming down her face. It was clear to me I was not going to get an answer to my question. Or, maybe I had in fact gotten an answer to my question. Yes, on some level, conscious or not, she had chosen what she thought John could provide over me having my father. This was about what was best for her, not what was best for me.

"At some point, I attached myself to Ed as my father. I recall asking if I could go with Mark and Mandy to his house before they moved to Alaska. Was that the transition, or was there any actual conversation about it between you and Ed or you and Mark and Mandy?"

"You know, I don't remember. I think you went to their house in Bellevue before they moved to Alaska, but I'm not sure. But no there was no official conversation. It just sort of evolved."

I opened my mouth to speak, and she cut me off defensively.

"And no, I didn't sit down and decide, 'will this be better for Syd or worse for Syd?' she said with sarcasm in her voice.

"I just did the best I could at the time. And you were a very happy-go-lucky-kid. So, I also didn't have any reason to be worried about you. You were just very happy all the time."

"OK," I said to try and show her I was accepting what she was saying. "I agree. I would characterize myself as a happy kid, but with some very odd quirks." She looked at me warily. "I had a vicious temper — that is usually the result of trauma in a child. And I had a lot of irrational fears. I imagined there was an entire world of tiny people who lived under my bed, who every night were trying to crawl up my bedspread and cut off my feet, so I'd bleed to death. My coping mechanisms were that they could only come out if it was totally dark and they were so tiny, they couldn't travel all the way to my feet before morning. But every morning, the first thing I did when I woke up was check to see if my feet were still on. And I kept all this hidden from everyone. Well, not the anger part. I attacked plenty of people. But I have been really good at swallowing and shoving all of this down such that you'd have to be paying attention to know anything was wrong with Syd."

"So you're saying I wasn't paying attention?"

"No, I'm agreeing with you. I was, for the most part, a happy kid, but there were clear signs that all was not well." She just looked at Jack still mercifully sleeping on the floor at my feet. I knew we were running out of time before one of the girls would be up or he'd need to be fed, so I forged on. "We mentioned Alaska. Clearly, Ed was not my dad, so why did you send me up there for a month to visit him?"

"I had no intention of sending you. I thought you'd get to the airport and be too scared to go and then I'd bring you back home with me. I had it all worked out that you'd stay with Grandma Rhodes while I was at work some of the time, and

211

with the neighbors some of the time. But then, when we got there," she laughed to herself in some amazement, "you couldn't have been more excited. It was Mandy who was scared and didn't want to go. I had to get Mark to distract you so I could talk to her. Finally, I talked her into getting on the plane and had to scramble to buy you a last-minute ticket. Then they had to re-arrange seats so you could be in Mark's seat by Mandy and he had to sit a few rows back by himself. I couldn't believe you."

"Back to my original question. Why did you send me to spend a month, in Alaska, a plane ride away, with someone who is not my father?" She took a drink of her water and looked out the window.

"Listen, you want to second guess every decision I made as a parent, go ahead. I did the best I could. I wasn't perfect, I never said I was. You wanted to go with your brother and sister, so I let you. Why is that so horrible?"

"OK, that's fine, but do you have any idea how horrible they were to me while I was there? Do you know they went out of their way to make sure I knew how little I mattered to them or at all? And all the while, I was fully convinced — why wouldn't I be — that was my dad telling me I didn't matter, not to him, not at all. That was devastating." And I took a deep breath and drink of my water. With clouded eyes, I blinked a few times to look at my notes. When it became clear she wasn't going to answer or say anything, I steeled my resolve and took a deep breath to try and calm my rising emotions. "I have just one more question."

"What else could you possibly have to say?"

I swallowed hard and forged ahead, "Why did you wait so long after Gus was back in our lives to tell me he is my dad?"

"Because I didn't want to upset you. Our lives had finally settled down and become peaceful. John left. Mandy left. Mark was in Germany. It was just you and me, and you were doing great. I was afraid if I gave you such dramatic news right in the middle of adolescence, it could throw you into a tail spin, and I didn't want that. I kept telling myself when she's sixteen, but then that would come and I'd think, no, she's doing so well, I don't want to upset her. OK, when she graduates from high school, but that came, and you were heading off to college and that seemed hard enough. But then you were getting married and I could see that it bothered you that Ed wasn't coming to your wedding and I didn't want you to have that dark cloud over your wedding. I wanted you to know that your dad was going to be there. I thought you were ready for it."

I cleared my throat to speak, but she cut me off, "And I was right. It was very upsetting to you and any earlier in your life would have been too hard on you. Syd, I want you to know I love you very much and I have never wanted to hurt you. I always tried to do my best for you. I did the best I could at the time. I'm sorry if you have been hurt. I'm sorry for all of it, but I did my best."

"Mommy, is Granma here?" Mia's voice called from the stairway.

"Yes, Mia, she's here. Would you like to come down and see her?"

"Yay, Granma." And we heard little feet scampering down the stairs and hallway. She rounded the corner into the family room as my mom wiped her eyes and got up to open her arms to Mia running toward her. I stood up to block Jack sleeping on the floor from Mia's single-minded running so she wouldn't trample him on her way to hug her much loved grandma.

The little bell that clung to the top of the door on Jimmy's Chinese Restaurant made me wonder if it was a restaurant or the goat in my grandparents' neighbor's yard as I opened the door to the twilight lit little place that smelled of garlic and chili sauce. I was still exhausted from my conversation with my mom that afternoon, but I knew I needed to do this before I lost my nerve and hid it all behind a smile like one of Shakespeare's fools thinking a simple masquerade mask could hide her true identity like I had been doing my entire life. Gus was sitting at the booth back by the kitchen, which would give us as much privacy as possible, but also would make it hard to hear him because his voice always ran out of breath about midway through his sentences.

He stood up to greet me with a half hug as I slid quickly into the booth, "Hey Syd, I'm so glad you called. I've been wanting to talk to you for years about this."

"Why haven't you then?" I startled both of us with my direct question.

"Well, I wasn't sure you were ready."

"You know, I think everyone has been leaving way too much up to me in this whole matter. Sure, I'm an adult now, but let's just operate on the premise that I'm the child in this situation who needs to be taken care of by her parents. And so far, my overarching feeling is that I have not been." I took a deep breath and told myself to try and not take out on him what I was feeling from my conversation with my mom. It wouldn't be easy.

"OK, fair enough." And he paused, not so much so I could see the pain register on his face, but it was as quick and clear as a flash of lightning across a summer evening sky. "In that case, I'll tell you what I know, what happened from my

214

perspective. But feel free to stop me, ask what you want, interrupt at any time and make sure you're getting what you need."

And all I could do was nod for the lump in my throat was already too big to speak around.

Just then a delightful Chinese man appeared beside our table. "You know what you order? Special good!"

Gus said, "We'll have chicken chow mien, almond fried chicken, orange chicken, and brown rice, please. And we'll need forks to eat with," brushing the chopsticks that were on the table aside.

"OK, lot of food," he replied.

"Yeah, well she's kinda a pig," Gus joked. I didn't laugh, so everyone was just confused. After a long, awkward pause, the waiter asked,

"Drink?"

"Just water for me," I managed.

"Yes, just water for both of us," Gus echoed.

"OK, right away."

And he left us to our misery.

"You know your mom and I weren't married when we had you. But oh, how I loved you."

"I gather she was separated from Ed, and you were married to Diane, is that right?"

"Yes, that's right. You came to work with your mom every day, and honestly, you were the light and air in my world."

"How old was I when you left Diane?"

"Um, let's see." I could tell my direct questions were flustering him a bit, and that he didn't expect this line of questioning, but I wanted to know the facts.

"Officially, we were separated after I was arrested, and

215

divorced after my trial, but we'll get to that. For all those years when you came to work with your mom, and I saw you every day, I, well, I just thought I could keep that going. I thought it could just stay that way for all of us. I should have done things different, but I didn't want to upset my mother more. She was so fragile by then. She really lost her mind after the Second World War. We're from the tiny island of Leros and the Nazis bombed it severely. Her parents were there, and her father was the priest on the island. Every day for fifty-five days, they bombed the island thinking everyone and everything would be destroyed. The book and movie, *The Guns of Navarone*, are about Leros, but anyway, my grandfather gathered everyone in his church and they prayed. The bombs bounced off the church and they were all fine. So, when the Germans finally landed on the island, they were shocked to find them all. So, they took the mayor and the priest and their wives and dragged them behind their tanks through the streets until they were barely alive. Then they buried them alive in a cave to die of starvation and their wounds. With their leaders gone, the people then submitted. After the war, my parents went back to have them taken from that cave and given a proper burial. My mother never recovered, and my brother and sister and I have been taking care of her and protecting her from anything that could upset her ever since. So, you see, I couldn't upset her with a divorce and," he paused and looked at his hands.

"And with a bastard child?" I asked. "Did she ever know I exist?"

His voice was softened by sadness and regret as he answered, "I don't know if you can understand that, but I just didn't think she could take it, she just wasn't strong enough."

Just then our food arrived. Plate after plate of steaming

Chinese food. The sweet man smiled at us and said, "Here you go, you food. So good. So much for the pig." And Jimmy laughed at his joke. We tried to laugh with him, but it was forced and he felt bad. "Need anyting?" We just shook our heads and started scooping food onto our individual plates. Moving it around would give us something to do with our hands.

"But then, when you were five, things started going bad between your mom and me. She got a new job and I didn't see you anymore. My mom got real sick. She was in the hospital and was dying. The two most precious people to me were gone. Every day I would go to the hospital and watch her suffer and slip away and I couldn't do anything. I'd donate blood as often as they let me, but it didn't help. I got all my friends to donate blood in her name, but it didn't help. I was losing my mind. Really, having a nervous breakdown because I was so powerless to help. Then, my mom died. She had never even met you and I'd lost both of you.

"I wore her hospital bracelet until they took it from me and threw it away. At her funeral, I put your pre-school picture in her casket so she could know you from heaven. You would have loved my mom. She was very religious like you are. She used to fast for forty days of lent just like Jesus did when he was in the desert. But anyway, I was in a really bad place. And I had been helping my friend, Chief Glant, with the Lynnwood Police try to catch some bad cops. They figured out it was me and they were trying to retaliate and had been watching me for an opportunity. They knew your mom left me and took you with her. They knew my mom died. And they saw that as their opportunity. They hired someone to come to me and tell me John was abusing you and that they'd kill him for me. They'd help me protect you. I said do it. I couldn't do anything to help my mom, but I was gonna do what I could to help you. I wasn't gonna stand by and let you be hurt when I could do something. So, I said do it. I wasn't in my right mind, but to be honest, if I knew someone was hurting you or one of your kids, I'd do whatever I could to protect you, even now.

"I didn't know I was being set up. So, I met the guy back at The Lynnwood a few hours later, gave him my shot gun and half of one thousand dollars. I gave him eight one-hundred-dollar bills and four fifty-dollar bills, but I tore them in half and gave him half then and I was gonna give him half when he killed John so he couldn't hurt you anymore.

"That night was awful. I was waiting and waiting, couldn't sleep. I was so torn between guilt and wanting to stop it and wanting it to be over so you'd be safe. Early the next morning, I was sitting at my desk and the police showed up. I was so relieved. They came bursting through my office door, slamming it off the wall like a hockey puck. Four officers aimed their guns at my head.

'Are you Gus Nick Papadakis?'

"It was surreal up to then. Relief melted through me when I looked into the officers' faces. I didn't have to keep this going anymore.

"It was like the Rockford Files, sort of. They said, 'Keep still and put your hands where we can see them! Gus, you are under arrest for the attempted murder of John Rossler', and they read me my rights.

"I said, 'Yes'. But all I could think of was they said 'attempted'. Thank God it didn't work. No one died!

"After searching and handcuffing me, they took hold of my arms tighter than was necessary and dragged me out to the car, even though I was willing to walk. I was still so overwhelmed with relief that they said attempted murder. Somehow the plan failed, John was alive, and I was glad for it. They threw me in the back seat. And when they got me to the police station, they took everything from me and put it in an envelope — except my mother's hospital bracelet. The officer just threw that away. It took everything in me not to cry at that.

"Next, the four officers took me in the elevator. No one had spoken to me other than to tell me where to sit and stand since we left my office. With a nod from the large man, another officer reached out and purposefully pushed the stop button on the elevator control panel. Before I could even turn my head, a black sack smothered my sight and breathing. The first blow came from behind and buckled my knees. It was followed by a solid punch to my stomach, which left me doubled over. Then they took turns raining down punches, kicks, and blows to every part of my body. They threw me against the wall repeatedly. I thought they were going to kill me. But they were smart. They bruised every part of my body, but they didn't break anything. When they finally stopped, I was spitting blood, couldn't walk, or hardly breathe. They jerked me to my feet, took off the sack and started the elevator up again."

"They took me down a long hall past many full cells of hooting and hollering criminals. 'Hey, what happened to him?'.

'He going to die?'.

'Throw him in here, let us have a crack at him'.

'Man, you in bad shape'.

"Then they stopped in front of a cell, opened the door, took off my handcuffs and threw me to the floor.

219

'Oh man, you in real trouble now. You think you been beat, now you got to deal with Shorty. He's as mean as they come'.

'That boy gonna die tonight'.

'You better not bleed on his cell floor, he don like no messy cell'.

"I could hear them yelling, but I couldn't make sense of what they were saying. My ears were ringing. I saw black spots above my head when I dared to open my eyes. My breath was shallow. It hurt to take too much air in or to move any part of my body so I just laid there the way I landed when they threw me. Finally, someone got up off the bottom bunk and walked over to me.

"He said, 'You all right? I don't think I've seen them beat anybody that bad before. Man, I don't I think I've seen somebody beat that bad since my step daddy stopped beating my mamma. Hey, whatever your name is up there, you get down and let him have your bunk. I don't know what you did, but you must have really pissed them off. Anybody done something to piss them off that bad deserves a bunk'.

"The man from the top bunk jumped down and went to find a place on the floor. I didn't think I could get up on the top bunk, but I had the sense that if the man up there jumped down and took the floor with no questions at this man's order, I'd better try. But I couldn't get up.

"'OK, you're too busted up to get up there so I'll climb and you take the bottom for now. But you listen up good, as soon as you can move you're on the top, you hear?'.

"I just groaned in agreement and then the man lifted me onto the bottom bunk where I lay until breakfast the next morning. I tried to eat, but couldn't make my mouth move.

Plus, I didn't even want to think about digesting food, so I set it aside. I was arraigned and bail was set at seventy-five thousand dollars, but there was no money for it.

"I was in jail for several months waiting for my trial. My beating had somehow softened Shorty's heart the first night in my cell. I think I reminded Shorty of his mother and he wanted to take care of me the way he couldn't take care of her.

"It was clear to me that Shorty held some clout in that jail that I didn't understand but other inmates avoided and respected him. Nobody messed with him, and I mean nobody. The man who was sleeping on the top bunk the night I arrived wasn't there long, but he never mentioned the fact that he was sleeping on the floor, and I had his bunk. Shorty said it, and that was it. The officers who arrested me had the guards put me in that cell on purpose. They thought Shorty would give me a hard time and could even kill me. Men had died in his cell before. My friendship with Shorty angered them so they pitted other inmates against me. One man even threatened my life.

"I really thought I was in trouble. He could easily rape, beat, or kill me. The guards were behind the trouble so they arranged for him to be alone in the shower and threw me in there. Knowing all, Shorty learned what was up and helped me. He had a small blade he gave me and taught me how to use it most effectively. When the guards came to get me for the 'shower', I took my blade with me. They threw me in there, shut the door and left. Sure enough, my new friend was there too. When I showed him the blade and told him what I was prepared to do with it, he believed me. He knew Shorty was behind my getting the blade and knowing what to do with it, and he left me alone.

"So, anyway, the court had me evaluated to see if I was sane, if I could use an insanity defense. I was no help at all. My attorney was trying to find a way to get me off, or at least a lighter sentence, but I didn't have it in me to even fight for myself. I knew in my heart I committed the crime and I was so depressed, I wasn't sure I wanted to go back to a life without you, your mom, and without my mom. I didn't have any money to mount an investigation and a defense, so it wasn't looking good for me. Plus, the evidence was really bad. They had my shotgun and the torn bills — both halves. But in the end, they found me innocent by reason of entrapment because the crime was conceived of in the minds of the police. My attorney found enough evidence to prove they came to me with the idea that John was abusing you and with a plan to kill him; I didn't seek someone out. I really thought I was going to prison for a long time. When the jury came back in, I unclasped my watch and was handing it to my sister.

"But even though I was found innocent, I couldn't see you. Your mom and John didn't want me around, as you can imagine. It broke my already broken heart to lose you." He paused for a moment and looked up at me, then went back to pushing his food around.

I was getting angrier by the moment. Did he really think I wanted to hear about Shorty? But I couldn't speak for the lump in my throat. I was beginning to think this was a horrible idea.

"You haven't said a word in quite a while. I thought you had some questions?"

I swallowed, hard, three or four times, trying to get to a place where I could speak past the boulder that had grown at the back of my throat. I had lost a lot of the wherewithal I had talking to my mom. Plus, I just knew my mom a lot better, and

I found myself a little nervous. Jimmy rounded the corner from the kitchen to come and check on us. Our eyes met. Mine filled to the brim with tears that started to spill down my cheeks and he quickly moved to another table. I tried to speak but just shook my head and shrugged my shoulders, so he went on.

"Then, when I got out of jail, I had lost everything. The taverns were struggling before I was arrested, and with me gone for a few months, well, I had to declare bankruptcy and they were gone. I lived with my sister for a while and slowly got my feet back under me. It took years before I was in a place to start the pull tab business I had when I met you guys again."

"Well, I guess I know what happened to you now, but I had this naive notion that you'd be wondering about my experience growing up without you," I managed. "And then there are the years when you were a part of our lives dating mom when you guys obviously knew you're my dad, but I didn't. I still had to wade through life with no dad. Having you watch my games, escort me at homecoming, and sit at my graduation, could have meant my dad had finally arrived. But it didn't. To me then, you were just another in a long line of substitutes trying to fill a massive void. I imagine it was vastly different for you, yet you left me in that dark place trying to make the best of it. Mom said she didn't want to upset me in the middle of adolescence, but believe me, I was already upset. I'm just really good at hiding it." And I pursed my tiny lips out as far as I could. He just stared back at me looking defeated. "But what is really running through my mind, I'm not sure you want to hear. Because what you might not know about me is that I used to have quite a struggle with anger — I mean I'd really lose it. Not often, but when we were going through it growing up — you know stuff like John tormenting and *actually* abusing me to the point of breaking, or when Mandy ran away, you know looking back now, when we *were* taken into police custody, I'd lose my shit. One time, I chased a girl with a bat and if I caught her, I was threatening to kill her. But don't worry, Mom caught me before I caught her. And right now, I think you might expect me to feel bad for you. To feel some empathy for what you went through. And sure, I do. I really do. But I gotta be honest. I'm also really pissed. This... this." And I paused for a long time. "Well, I hope and pray this is the depths of my soul because what I see here is utter sludge. Thick, black sludge that right now feels a lot like quick sand. I'm mad that I had to grow up with John torturing me day in and day out; with Ed, who I thought was my dad, making sure I knew loud and clear, he couldn't give a rat's ass about my existence — that is on the rare occasion that we even saw him, while you were off being dad to Nick and Christine. Why did they get to have a dad and I didn't?" With that, I threw the fork that I'd destroyed by bending each prong backward and the handle into thirds onto the pile of shards I'd already broken my chopsticks into. We just stared at each other. I picked up his chopsticks and started into them.

Finally, Gus broke the silence. "I'm really sorry, Syd. I did love you, and I did the best I could. I know it wasn't great for you, but they wouldn't let me come around. And I don't know how going back will help us move forward."

"You see, that doesn't help either. You say you loved me, and you did your best. That's what Mom says. But I don't see it that way. That's not how I understand love. Love is not feeling good about someone and wanting good things for them, especially when they are your child. And you cannot do your best for them. You have to do what they require, what they need, no matter what it takes from you. That's the way I see love. That's what my faith has taught me. Love requires doing what is best for the other person, not some feeling and what you can muster. See, I think you guys acted in your best interests, every step of the way. Not mine. Never mine. You protected yourselves, not me, never me. Why didn't you give me your name? Why didn't you insist on seeing me? Some sort of custody? It sounds like that would have been messy for your life? For your other family — for your wife and other kids and for your mom and dad and sister. So that was better for you, but what was it for me? So, am I selfish now? Do I want only what's best for me? These are things children shouldn't have to decide, demand from their parents. It was a hard time. I get it. This is a hard time for me. Unbelievably hard. But I have three babies at home. And they don't get it. They just need a mom who is present and taking care of them, every day from here into forever."

And silence hung between us, and I broke the chopsticks into shards.

"And please, please, for God's sake, stop telling me stories about when Nick and Christine were growing up and you how you guys used to go test drive cars and when you coached Nick's teams and you used to play freeway games and you always made Nick give her points, because he was better at the games than she was, and all the things dads do with their kids. Do you know how that makes me feel? You somehow found a way to be their dad. To see them all the time. But you couldn't be mine. You left me to be tormented and ground into the dirt by two abusive, raging alcoholics. Please don't continue to rub it in over and over. That's just not nice."

"I'm sorry, I didn't realize," he uttered.

"I figured."

After a long pause, I knew I had to end the conversation. It had disintegrated far enough. "Well, I don't know what the

225

way forward looks like. Growing up, when it was hard, I just kept getting up and living the next day, and eventually it got better. That, and my faith; that always helped. Forgive and pray, over, and over, and over, and over. But I might need some help this time. This sludge just feels real thick."

"Syd, you're the best person I know. You'll be just fine."

"Let's be honest, you don't know me that well. What is really inside me shocked you just now. I could see it on your face."

"You want box?" Jimmy interrupted.

"Sure, we'd love some boxes," Gus answered and started getting busy with fishing out his wallet to pay the bill.

"I need to go to the bathroom. Excuse me."

When I returned to the table, the check was paid, the plastic bag with bright red letters that said 'THANK YOU' filled with white boxes full of all our uneaten food was tied neatly and sitting on the edge of the table.

"Why don't you take the leftovers? You and Evan and the girls can eat it tomorrow."

"Sure. Thanks."

And we made our ways out to our respective cars. I wondered what good this did after all. I knew time would pass. No one would talk about this again if I didn't bring it up, and I didn't think I had the wherewithal for much more of the likes of this. A holiday or birthday would bring us all together, and we'd press on. This was mine to forge through. So, I whispered, "Please Lord, don't let my feet get cemented in this sludge. I need your help." And I drove home to start bath and bed time.

Chapter Nineteen

I hoped talking with my parents would give me answers to questions I hadn't even let myself formulate. But it didn't. If anything, it made things worse and I started to retreat within myself in ways that scared me a little. I felt like I was numb and outside myself, watching myself go through the motions of making breakfast, nursing Jack, reading stories, pushing swings, making cheese sandwiches, changing diapers, and bath time, but I was absent from it all. Rationally, I knew I had three babies who needed me to be present, but physically going through the motions took everything I had. And when they went to bed each night, for months after that day with my mom and dinner with my dad, so did I.

One night Evan came in and sat beside me and gently rubbed my back. After a while of me just lying there he said, "Where have you gone?"

"I'm right here," I said not rolling over to look at him, pretending I didn't know what he was really asking.

"Syd," he said softly. "I miss you. I can't help you with this if you won't let me in."

"I'm just tired is all," I lied.

"You need to talk about this. If not with me, maybe with a counselor."

That got my attention. I gave him a hard look. "Do you have any idea how hard it is to take care of three kids under the age of three all day, every day?" I stared straight into his green eyes but he wouldn't look away. "Huh?" I added for emphasis.

"We both know how hard it is to take care of them. But we both know you need to talk about the genetic tests and your conversations with you parents. That is what this seven forty-five bed time you've adopted is all about."

"OK, fine. You want to talk about it? Let's talk about it. What do you think?"

"I think you're reeling from the news and you need to put into words how you feel rather than shove it down. You are choosing this dark road. And you are choosing to walk down it by yourself."

Now he was just pissing me off. I started to struggle to sit up but he was sitting on the blankets so I was a bit pinned. He noticed me trying to get up and moved, I thought so I could move. But instead, he pulled up the covers skootched me over and lay down beside me. That surprised me, and I lost a little steam, but not much.

"Listen, I warned you," I started back in.

He cut me off, "Yes, I recall that. You also asked me to remind you when it's time to pop the plate and clean out the hair clog."

I opened and closed my mouth a few times. Tears were streaming out the corners of my eyes and all I wanted him to do was leave me alone. When I felt like this growing up, I could do it. Smile all day long. Keep my grades up. Play my sports. And hide in my room or closet and no one bothered to check on me. I had never shared a room with anyone before, let alone a bed. And he was bothering me. As I turned to say 'after what I've been through, you have no right to say that to me', I heard that same voice that spoke to me on the side of the lake whisper to me, "He's right, you know." My words and breath caught hard in my throat. And he lay there beside me waiting.

Eventually, he lifted up my head and pulled it over on his chest. He kissed the crown of my head and said softly, "If you walk down this dark road for the rest of your life, I'll walk with you. But I think there's a better way."

I just nodded.

"I'll find us a counselor to go to together, how about that?"

I just nodded.

Chapter Twenty

After years of being inundated with babies and wading through the sludge, Evan and I decided we were going to have some fun that summer. Jack was not quite two, Skye just three, and Mia well past four, but not yet five. We set out to a little cabin we rented that sat on the edge of the Columbia River in Eastern Washington. There was a pool and playground set in between the orchards, and we were determined to enjoy ourselves.

Our first day proved promising. I rose early to spend some time enjoying the quiet and the river before boats and jet skis tore through its persistent current. There's something inspiring about rivers; they are always moving — in, around, and through whatever comes in their path. If it's too heavy, it sinks to the bottom and the water perseveres over it. If light, it is swept up and carried along. Not even stable mountains can withstand the cutting determination of a river. As I sat on the deck of our cabin watching the dark brown cliffs on the opposite bank lose their sunrise glow, an earth-shaking sound sliced through my serenity. They were so fast I would have never seen them fly by if I hadn't been sitting there watching. They were gone before the roar of their supersonic engines shook the deck and cabin behind me, my chest cavity along with them. Not much gets Evan up that early in the morning, but knowing his love for fighter jets, I knew he'd want to see them.

Of course, my excitement played me the fool as I went to

wake them. Nobody inside was still asleep after that noise and they soon joined me on the porch to watch the fighter jets from the Whidbey Island Naval Station skim above the river and cut through the canyon. The F-14s put on quite a show for us, even tipping their wings to our waves, each still in our jammies. Evan was thrilled, but went back to sleep after they left. The kids were terrified of the thunderous noise, and were definitely up for the morning.

With our early awakening and a few hours of swimming already exhausting his tiny body, Jack needed a nap before lunch. Evan stayed at the cabin with him while I took the girls out for a walk in the nearby apricot orchard. The fruit was heavy on the branches, its sweet ripening giving way to gravity.

Skye was hunched over a rotting pit, examining it like it held the secret to cold fusion when she finally said, "I jus don wike it. Too messy."

"Yep," I agreed, "it is certainly messy, little love, but it's necessary. If it has a shot at growing into a new tree, it has to rot away the mess first."

"But den, it's a twee?" She wanted to know the rotting mess would guarantee life. She asked emphatically without ever taking her doe-sized brown eyes from the rotting flesh.

"No, sorry love. Not every pit makes it into a tree. Some of them just keep rotting and rotting."

Mia jumped next to us capturing a grasshopper under her little hands. "I got it! What keeps rotting?"

"Got what?" Skye asked.

"A grasshopper. It's tickling me. But what keeps rotting?"

"These apricot pits that fell from the tree. We were just talking about how some of them can become trees and some just keep rotting and rotting."

"The lucky ones get to be a tree?" Mia asked. But then the grasshopper escaped from between her thumb and hand and she bounded off to capture it again.

Skye was still engrossed with the pit.

"Uck!" And with that she hit the ground with the stick she had in her hand and looked at me, frustrated. But in a flash, her face softened and she asked, "Mom?"

"Yes, love?"

"Can we hab a pobicle?"

Smiling at her ability to move from a philosophical plane to disgust to popsicles, I answered, "Sure, sweetheart, it's pretty hot, let's go get a popsicle."

Jumping from her crouch without a thought to stiff muscles, she bounded off, shouting to Mia, "Me, Mom says we can hab a pobicle," with enough enthusiasm to think she had, in fact, solved cold fusion.

Watching them run ahead to the cabin, Skye's full diaper swinging behind her, I thought, it's not luck that gets you through the rotting. It's not luck at all. It's knowing you're loved, and having the will of a river.

Epilogue
Sydney, Age 47

"Hey, Mia. How are you?"

"I'm good, Mom. You?"

"Same, good. How were your shifts this week?"

"Oh, they were good. The baby I'm taking care of is turning the corner. She had surgery on her heart and her intestines and both went really well. She's up to almost three pounds now."

"Oh that's amazing. I'm so happy to hear that.

"How's her mom holding up?"

"She's doing OK. She's just so young, I'm not sure she really understands how seriously ill her baby is. She just sits there on her phone the whole time."

"Is she gonna keep custody of her?"

"I don't know. It's still up in the air as to whether or not they'll let her. Taking drugs when you're pregnant is child abuse, so technically, they can take her away. The dad is nowhere to be found. I think they might be looking for family to take care of her, but she'll be in the hospital for so long, I don't think they have to figure that out yet."

"Well, I'm just happy the baby is getting stronger."

"For sure. What's up? Did you call to check on my patient?"

"Oh, no, well yes, But I also have some sad news. Papou's brother, George, died and the service is next week."

"Oh, that's too bad. I bet Papou is real sad about that."

"Yeah, I bet he is. I haven't talked to him. Grandma called me. He's been in and out of the hospital a lot for the last six months, and really in poor health, so I don't think it was a surprise, but still sad, nonetheless."

"Well, I'll call Papou."

"That's very sweet of you. He'll really appreciate that."

"Have you ever met him?"

"I've seen him twice, but it didn't go well."

"What do you mean, it didn't go well?"

"I saw him once at the restaurant and once at the hospital when Papou's kidneys weren't working. He looked at me and said, 'who's that and why is she here?'. It was very awkward."

"Oh Mom, I'm sorry. I saw him a bunch of times when I worked for Grandma and Papou at their restaurant. He didn't seem like a nice man. Is there a service?"

"Yes, Grandma says the service is going to be at The Greek Orthodox Church next Thursday at eleven. Do you know where that is?"

"Nope, I'm guessing downtown somewhere."

"Actually, it's in the University District somewhere, probably not far from where Jack and Skye live."

"Do you want all of us to go?"

"To be honest, I'd rather eat a bowl full of spiders than go, but Grandma said it would mean a lot to Papou if we went."

"Oh God, Mom, no need to be so violent. So, you're saying we should go?"

"Yes, I'm saying, I think we should go."

"OK, let me look and see if I have the night before off. Yes, I have the night before and that night off work. I'll call Jack and Skye and let them know."

234

"Thanks, but I can call them."

"No worries. I plan to talk with them today anyway."

"OK, sounds good. I think Jack just has class early on Thursdays, so he should be OK to go, but Skye may have to miss a class to go."

"I'm sure she won't mind. Besides, if I know Skye, she already has all of the work done for the rest of the quarter."

"Yep, you're right about that."

"They're on my way, so I can pick up Skye from her house and Jack from his frat, and we can meet you there."

"OK, I'll be coming from work, and Dad will be coming from work, so let's all try to be there about ten fifty so we walk in together. I do not want to show up there alone."

"Well, you better tell Dad to get there at ten thirty then."

"Yes, of course, I'll adjust Dad's arrival time. OK, thanks, love. I appreciate your help with this."

"Absolutely, Mom. We love you, and we love Papou. We will be there."

The raindrops were so thick they felt like a swarm of locusts that would devour my car as I sat outside the Greek Orthodox Church in the University District watching the minutes eek by. Ten fifty-four beamed at me from my dashboard, but I still hadn't seen either Evan or Mia, Jack, and Skye arrive. I texted them all asking if they were close, but no one had replied. Frustrated and nervous, I took a deep breath, cracked open my door just enough to poke my umbrella out and open it above me before I pushed the door the rest of the way open and stepped out into the deluge. Even though I was under my umbrella, I instinctively ducked my head and shoulders as I ran across the street, jumping over the massive puddles on my way to the large, golden domed church. I had, of course, never been to the church where only members of the Greek Orthodox religion attend. Why would I have been? As I opened the large wooden door, ornately carved with scenes from the gospels, I pulled my umbrella closed and shook off as much water as I could. Much to my relief, the first four faces I saw were Evan, Jack, Mia, and Skye's. They were waiting just inside for me.

"Hey, where did you guys' park? I've been out front watching for you."

"In the parking lot. We've been waiting for you."

"Oh, I didn't know there was a parking lot."

"Skye knew where it was from the time she came here with Papou, a few years ago."

"Oh, that's right. I forgot about that."

Just then, my mom came up to greet us. "Here, let me get your coats and take that wet umbrella. I can hang them on the coat rack."

"Hey, Grandma," Jack said as he hugged her.

"Oh, hi, honey. It's so good for you all to come. It will make Papou so happy."

Something about my mom's presence made me nervous, so as she took my coat and umbrella and continued greeting and hugging my family, I slid a few feet away. Just then, my dad tapped me on the shoulder and said, "Syd, I'm so glad you made it. Let me introduce you to my niece, Lauren."

I turned to follow him as he greeted a beautiful young woman of about twenty standing a few feet behind me.

"Syd, this is my niece, Lauren. She is Jeff's daughter. You know, Jeff is Iris's son, so Lauren is Iris's granddaughter. She is studying in Los Angeles."

"Hello, Lauren, it's very nice to meet you," I said, shaking

Lauren's hand.

"Lauren, this is Syd. She's…" and he paused and looked from me to her and back again. "She's…" And he paused again and looked off behind Lauren at the crowd that had gathered inside the church. Lauren and I looked at each other uncomfortably. She had no idea who I was and she looked expectantly at my dad to tell her who I was the same way he had told me who she was. But he just stammered uncomfortably. "Hey, Lauren, did I ever tell you that I was the best man in your parents' wedding?"

"Huh, no, Uncle Gus. I didn't know that." And Lauren looked at me apologetically.

"Excuse me, Lauren. It was nice to meet you, but I think I'll go find my seat now." And I walked away without even meeting my dad's gaze. I'm sure it was downcast in either embarrassment, or shame, or both.

I quickly made my way to the second to last pew and sat down. My breath was quick and shallow as I tried to make sense of why he had called me over to introduce me to her and then refused to tell her who I am. Was he ashamed of me? I'm not sure how long I sat there before Evan, Mia, Jack, and Skye sat down beside me.

"Hey, you OK?" Evan whispered.

"No, I don't think so," I whispered back. As I looked over at him, all three kids were looking straight at me with concern on their faces. "My dad just refused to tell his niece who I am. He totally froze and changed the subject like he's completely embarrassed to admit I'm his daughter." They all looked at me confused. But before I could say much more, the music started and the processional began.

We rose to our feet to watch George's casket be carried in

by all of his great nephews, including my half-sister, Christina's two boys. Next, his wife and two adult children followed. Behind them came Papou's sister — Iris and her entire family, including her husband adult children and their children, Lauren among them. Following the youngest of Iris's grandchildren were my parents, arm in arm, then my dad's two children, Nick and Christine, and Nick's daughter. Christine's boys weren't there, of course, because they had helped carry the casket. The air left me as my mom looked over at me with an apologetic smile. I sat down under the puzzled and angry looks of my three children. In my mind, I started a conversation with Mrs. B. "You know, Mrs. B, turns out, moms can turn on you too." And I pictured myself in my childhood closet with Cocoa and a bright blue box of milk bones; a litany of swear words ran through my mind. I had lost track of where I was until I felt Evan's arm around my shoulder. As I looked over at him and the kids behind him, I realized I was actually sobbing. When my mind rejoined my physical body back in the pew in the back of the church, I began to shake. When the line of priests chanting and waving incense had finally made their way in, we got up and left.

Out in the lobby, Jack said, "What kind of bullshit was that?"

"I, I don't even know. Before the service even started, Papou wouldn't tell his niece who I was. He just made up some distraction about him being in her parents' wedding. They're ashamed of me."

"Well, they are the ones who should be ashamed of themselves," Jack said again. "This is just bullshit."

Mia and Skye said, almost in unison, "I'm so sorry, Mom."

"I'll be all right. Just give me a moment, but I'll be all right. But I just might need a moment."

Jack, Evan, and Skye went to find the bathroom before we left. Standing in the foyer, Mia said, "I'll go get our coats and your umbrella." When I was there by myself, I looked in the sanctuary at my family sitting together in the first two rows of pews. The back of my parents' heads beside Nick and Christine's heads lined up beside their children's heads seemed to scream at me. I had to get out of that church, so I opened the door and ran through the pelting rain to my car. As I slammed the car door against the storm outside, my phone vibrated in my pocket. Mia was calling me.

"Hi, love."

"Mom, where did you go?"

"I'm in my car."

"OK, but why didn't you wait for me. I have your coat and umbrella. You must be soaked."

"I'm sorry, I just had to get out of there."

"Mom, we're all here. You don't need to drive yourself home. We were talking about getting lunch before you got here. Let's all go get some lunch. It'll make you feel better."

"Thanks, love, but I don't want to sit in public right now. I need some time. You guys go ahead. I'll be fine." And I hung up.

As I sat there with my head tilted back against the seat trying to breathe in and out slowly, my phone vibrated again. It was Evan.

"Hello."

"Hey girl."

"Hey."

"I want you to come to lunch with us."

"I know you do, but listen to me. I am in no shape to be out in public right now. And I need some time to process this. And I do not want to do it in front of the kids. They should not have to take care of me. I mean it. Kids should not have to take care of their parents. I've made them do that before, and they hate it. I will not do that with this. They get to be kids, and I will be the grown up. It's just right now, I need a bit of time and space and I might not do the best job of that, so I need you to take them to lunch and give me that space. Can you do that for me? Please don't let them try to take care of me. That's not what kids should have to do. Plus, I don't want to ruin their relationship with their grandparents. They may be shitty parents right now, but they've been really good grandparents. Let's leave them that. It's just too raw right now."

"Yeah, yeah, yeah, I get all that, but the best thing for you is to be with us right now."

"Will you please listen to me? I'm not going to sit in a restaurant right now. I'm barely keeping myself together. But I am, OK. Or, I will be."

"OK, I'll come with you. Are you headed home?"

"Yeah, I'm headed home, but really, can I have a bit of time? You have lunch with the kids. If you come with me, they'll come with me. I need you to listen to me." He was quiet for a minute, and I knew he was realizing I was right.

"Are you sure about this?"

"I am insisting on this. I know how to navigate this. I've done it before. I can do it again. I just need a moment, and I will be fine. Please trust me. I'll be OK."

"OK. We love you."

"I know. And I appreciate it very much. I love you."

And I hung up and drove home in a trance of shock.

As I entered the garage, I could hear my little dog, Lucy, barking her greeting. A smile curled the edges of my mouth ever so slightly. I made my way to my closet, her tiny feet bouncing off my calf with every step. I stripped off my wet clothes and left them in a pile on the floor. Rummaging through the laundry pile, I found my black fleece pants and sank into them. Next, I pulled my flannel night shirt off the hook and draped it over my head. On my way back to the family room, I stopped to grab some warm socks. I arranged the couch pillows and opened the lid to the storage ottoman to get the fleece blanket from Costco. Once I situated myself nicely into the pillows with my back nestled into the back of the couch and my head half buried in the pillows, I covered myself in the blanket and reached down to lift Lucy up so she could dig herself a perfect nest up against my stomach. No biscuits. No swearing. Just lying there wondering how I'd let them fool me twice. Every few minutes I'd find myself with tears running down my face, but they'd dry up as I'd get angry at myself for being such a fool. I actually thought I was safe and that I could trust them. Finally, I gave in to the emotions I'd been holding at bay, trying to muscle and brave my way through since running through the rain to my car and the first sob came out so unexpectedly and loud that Lucy jumped and started to shake. It was a long, ugly cry that took me back through all of the humiliation and hurt that I had long forgotten.

Exhausted, I drifted off to sleep. Lucy's barking and standing on my head to get to the back of the couch so she could see who was coming in the door woke me up. I heard the garage door closing and figured Evan was home. But then I heard Jack's voice and Skye's laugh. They were all here.

"Mom."

"Hey, Luce," Mia said in the high voice people use to talk to dogs as she made her way to pet Lucy.

I pushed myself up so they could see me on the couch. "Hey guys," I said.

"We brought you some food."

"Thanks. Where did you go, Mexican or Thai?" I asked.

"Why those guesses?" Evan asked.

"Because that's the only two places you ever want to go," I answered.

"She knows you," Jack chimed in.

By then, they'd all come into the family room and found a seat either on the couch or the ottoman.

"We got Mexican food," Skye finally answered. "We brought you a taco salad."

"Thanks guys. I really appreciate it."

"How're you doing?" Mia asked.

"I'm hanging in there," I said with a half-smile. "Mostly, I really feel like a fool. It's kinda like, fool me once, shame on you, fool me twice, shame on me."

"Well, I don't think you're a fool. If you can't trust your parents, who can you trust?" Jack said.

Everyone else gave him a scolding look. "Oh, man. That's not what I meant. I mean, you can trust us. We won't let you down."

"I know that, Jack. But you're right. If you can't trust your parents, it does call a lot into question. And I guess I thought, after all these years together being a family that it was good, but if that was an illusion, then I'd rather know where I stand than live in some kind of Pollyanna, la-la-land. But here's the thing. I'm not saying this will be easy, but I've learned this